Skid Marks

Charles E. Cravey

Published by:

6500 Clito Road
Statesboro, Georgia 30461 (U.S.A.)
(912) 587-4400

LIBRARY OF CONGRESS
CATALOGING-IN-PUBLICATION DATA

Cravey, Charles E
Skid Marks/Charles E. Cravey.

p. cm.
ISBN: 1-58535-165-2

Printed in the United States of America on acid-free paper.

Book Design by Charles E. Cravey

Acknowledgments

My thanks to the following who have
been more than kind to me in
my quest to write the great
American Novel:

Renee Cravey
Angela Blum
Jonathan Cravey

And to
Patsy Deloach and *Katheryn Wells*
for their diligent work of
editing.

"The courage of life is often a less dramatic spectacle than the courage of the final moment; but it is no less a magnificent mixture of triumph and tragedy."

John F. Kennedy

To Renee,

my wife,

my life

Chapter One
Death and Fate

How will it happen? Will it be one of those glorious mornings when everything in your life seems to be going great and then, without warning, you're blind-sided on the highway by a teenaged kid on his way to school who's late for class? Will it happen in the dead of night or early morning, when you're awakened by the sound of an intruder in your home who pulls the trigger in fright or haste? Or will it be after a long, lingering illness in a hospital with tubes in every vein, oxygen mask around your face, your family standing there holding your hands in a timeless vigil when you struggle for that last precious breath? Perhaps it'll happen after you've slipped into that dreaded Alzheimer's and then the peace comes quietly, suddenly one evening with only a staff nurse by your side, checking your pulse and calling out the time of death. Could it happen all of a sudden when that shooting pain in your right arm finally does signal a heart attack? Will you be busy at work, doing those things you enjoy, when the final warning is sounded, or will you be peacefully asleep in your warm and cozy bed at home?

I guess you get my drift by now. We have no idea how Death will invade our lives, and that's probably for the best. Can you imagine someone wanting to know the exact time, place, and reason for their death in advance? I'm afraid that most of us, with that kind of knowledge, wouldn't know how to respond. We'd become nervous wrecks, unable to function in a normal capacity. We'd be afraid to go to sleep at night for fear that we wouldn't awaken in the morning. Our every waking hour would be filled with apprehension and anxiety.

The truth of the matter is that we aren't given a timetable for those matters in advance, and that's for OUR good. We take our chances, day in, day out, living out our lives in hopes that Death will come much later when we're old and gray and are no longer of use to anyone. We move at a normal pace hoping that Death doesn't know our name or address.

So be it. It will happen one day, sooner or later, but I'll gladly take the later. Still, we are never assured of either. I guess it's somewhat like the Lottery: you place your bet, buy your card and scratch to see if you're a winner; only Death is more definite and final. There won't be another day to buy another chance to win. It's over, final, period! When your winning scratch comes up, the Grim Reaper has won!

My friend Hank Sessions had everything going for him. He was a highly successful lawyer in Atlanta with a firm that had just offered him a full partnership. He had accepted and was celebrating with his best friend Tom Sebring. They had taken a few days off and had headed down to Tarpon Springs on the Gulf Coast of Florida to fish offshore. They rented this nice little boat and had gone out about eight miles or so and had settled in to fish. After hooking a large fish and fighting to bring him in, Hank slipped and fell overboard with all of his gear. Tom immediately jumped in to rescue him, but developed cramps in both of his legs. He struggled to get back to the boat but lost sight of Hank in the process. With extreme pain in his legs, he managed to crawl back onboard. Looking all around the boat for signs of Hank, he became eerily aware that Hank had drowned in this great depth of water, and now he was alone.

He radioed in to the boat company and told them the dilemma while keeping his eyes focused on the dark waters of the Gulf. A chill settled into his body as the late evening came. He then began to realize the ultimate. "What am I going to tell his wife?" he wondered. "How will I be able to face everyone back at the firm with the news that Hank's not coming back? Everyone will be blaming me for his death! I don't know if I can take it or not."

The Coast Guard finally arrived on the scene after what seemed like an eternity for Tom. Their search for Hank's body continued into the night without luck. They carried Tom back to Tarpon Springs and on to the local hospital where he was checked and later released. He then called home and told Miriam, his wife, the tragic news and asked her to go over to Helen's (Hank's wife) house and stay with her until his return to Atlanta.

Long, weary days passed with no news from the Coast Guard. After two weeks, the search was canceled without results. "Life is just not fair," my dad used to say, "and then you die!" But whoever promised us that it would be fair? Did someone teach us early on that everything would always go OUR way? How stupid can we be to think that we're impervious to Death?

Or, take my old friend, Harry Martin. Harry was my father's best friend until my father's death six years ago to cancer. Harry was the finest Christian man you would ever meet. He was in church every time the doors opened and was the spearhead behind the annual Food Box campaign for the poor in the community. Every year he would successfully raise funds at church to purchase food boxes for the poor and needy. Last year alone (at $20 per box) he raised enough to purchase 433 boxes! That's amazing, but you just had to know the zeal and love of this guy to appreciate what I'm about to tell you.

Harry was out at the Linger-Long Golf Course one day with his friends and was having a fantastic game. He was leading the group of four men with a 6 under par when it happened. Out of the blue-clear sky came a golf ball from an adjoining tee that smacked Harry on the left side of his temple, sending him immediately to the ground with a hard thud. He squirmed and moved about before the other men and made a few muttering sounds before losing consciousness. The men were dumbfounded and one took off hurriedly back to the clubhouse to alert the golf pro of what had happened. Within minutes, an ambulance arrived, and the driver followed the golf cart path to where they were. After checking his pulse and vitals, they placed him on the stretcher and then into the ambulance and off to the local hospital. He was pronounced dead at the emergency room, suffering from an apparent hematoma to the brain. Harry was one of the greatest men I had ever known! Why? Why? Why? Does anyone know the answer?

Caldwell was in mourning over one of its exemplary citizens. Harry would not be forgotten for his devotion and friendship, his caring and loving spirit, and his faithfulness to everyone who knew him. What a tragedy to our little community! Again, no one knows what freak accident may one day become our destiny.

Last winter two hunters discovered the body of a young twenty-two year old black man partially covered by tin from an old home site out in the woods. His body had been there for three weeks or more, according to the county coroner, and the stench was overwhelming to the hunting dogs and the men who found him. The men summoned the EMS who quickly arrived and carried the body back to the local hospital. After extensive research by the county Sheriff, it was determined that he and his male lover in Chicago had a fight the night of his death, and his lover had knocked him out with a broom handle. The following morning, his lover discovered him still down on the floor and non-responsive. Out of fear for what he had done, he loaded the body into the trunk of his car and drove all the way from Chicago to Siler, Georgia, to his grandfather's old home site in the woods where he left the body underneath some rusty sheets of tin from the old home's roof. He then returned to Chicago and tried to act as though nothing had happened. Today he's serving a life sentence in the prison system of Illinois.

What a tragedy! Yet, it happens over and over again each day. Just when you think it's safe to get up, leave your home, and go to work, it can happen.

We could, of course, become paranoid (as some have) and never take a risk in life. But that would be self-defeating, wouldn't it? We have to trudge along and face the consequences of our lives with the confidence that to-day will be a great day and good things are going to happen!

Chapter Two
Seymour and John Maxwell

It was 1975, hot, humid and sticky outside. It was mid-day, and I was just finishing my final semester exam at Abraham Baldwin College in Tifton, Georgia. Excited to be completely through with my second year of college, I felt sure that I had aced the exam to finish my two-year degree at ABAC. I would then transfer to Valdosta State to complete my four-year course work in Sociology.

I pulled out of the college parking lot in my old 1972 blue Volkswagen Super Beetle and was headed back home to Seymour. I loved that old Volkswagen and had accumulated quite a number of miles on her. Seymour was approximately forty miles from Tifton and was a fairly small town with about 2,200 people. You know the kind—everybody knows everybody's business! Secrets aren't secrets very long before they are discovered. The saying is that you can tell one person at 8 AM a secret and by 5 PM that evening the entire town knows about it. It may have taken a few turns in its interpretation, but the basic secret is out! People have a love/hate relationship with these small towns, but living in a small town does

have its benefits for folks who enjoy the small town at-
mosphere, less traffic, a more leisurely way of life, and
being able to meet someone on the street that you actually
know. Seymour was that kind of town. People looked after each other when trouble came. We had a Baptist,
Methodist, Church of God and a Presbyterian congregation in Seymour. Church-life and events surrounding the
churches took up the majority of peoples' lives when they
were not at work. The pastors all worked together in a
ministerial association and planned such events as the annual Bar-B-Q to raise funds for the local Children's
Home; the school Baccalaureate Service, which rotated
from church-to-church each year; and the community
wide Revival in which a well-sought-after preacher from
out of town was invited to preach to all churches under the
Big-Tent.

     Seymour was thriving with a new pants factory. It
had just hired 220 new workers and had gone on-line a
couple of months ago. We had a peanut mill, a cotton gin,
a Five-and-Dime store, and rumors were that we were
about to get a McDonald's Restaurant! Everyone was excited about that and couldn't wait for those French fries
and hamburgers. We also had Seymour High School
(from which I graduated two years ago), Walton Middle
School (named after a World War II citizen of Seymour
who had died in service), and Seymour Elementary
School where my mother had been teaching Second Grade
for the past thirteen years. She loved her job and was totally devoted to her students. Mama had a habit of visiting

the homes of parents when their children were unruly at school. She made it a point each year to visit these homes and to learn as much as possible about their situations in the home environment. She felt that would give her a better handle on how to deal with each individual student. Other teachers were jealous of her, but loved her devotion and loyalty to the task. I guess we could use a bit more of that enthusiasm today on behalf of all teachers! The truth of the matter is that many teachers are simply tired of trying and have given up hope for their students. The classrooms are now cold and calculated. Education, and the pursuit of it, has taken a back row seat. Most of a teacher's day is spent dealing with discipline and the ever-evolving demands of the State Testing Curriculums. As soon as one benchmark is met, there are two more behind it to implement! It's a never-ceasing battle to keep one's head above water! Many teachers have left the classroom for other ventures in the secular world mainly because of such constant demands.

Mama was great with the kids and loved the art of teaching. Somehow she managed to follow the curriculum for her second grade, but also found time to do fun things with her kids. They all seemed to love her. She had been chosen three times as Teacher of the Year at Seymour Elementary. In fact, she had been chosen twice by the High School Star Student as Star Teacher, so she must have been doing something right! We were all so proud of her accomplishments.

Mama helped with the purchase of my new Volks-

wagen in Macon at Bray's VW. She had co-signed with
me on my first ever loan and had paid the down payment
of $200. It was then my responsibility to make the
monthly payments of $125. I would accomplish that with
my job in the evenings at the Star Theater in town, running the projector and occasionally working behind the
counter selling cokes, popcorn, and other goodies to the
customers. It gave me that much-needed discipline and
kept me humble when dealing with the public. James
Gray, the owner of the Star, had been a high school friend
of my father's. When I turned sixteen and in the Ninth
Grade I was offered the job by Mr. Gray, and immediately
accepted. He knew that I would be going to college in a
few years and would need money to help pay for it. I was
to come in at 5 PM each afternoon to assume my duties.
As soon as I had secured the position, I was able to con-
vince mom into signing with me for the VW. She gladly
obliged. That was five years ago, and I'm still driving my
dream car. Sundays usually finds me in the back yard
grooming the old VW with the utmost of care. She has
over 120,000 miles on her now, but she still runs like a
top! I keep the oil changed on a regular basis, and have
never had one lick of trouble with her. The only thing I
had wished for was an air conditioner! We were in the
deep south and the summers were intolerable. Driving in a
small car made it even more so. I would open both vents
and roll down both windows whenever I took her on the
road. I had made the final payment on her last September,
and mama took me out to celebrate the event since I had

managed to never miss a payment! She was very proud of me, and so was I.

Saturday nights at the theater were usually date-nights. Since the eighth grade, I had been seeing Missy Rhodes, a young beautiful redhead whose father was the owner of Rossy's Feed Mill in town. She was absolutely gorgeous and was also a good sport, spending those Saturday nights in the projection room with me. It didn't seem to bother her at all, as long as the two of us were together. Her parents didn't know about our relationship, however, so we had to slip around to see each other. She would go to the movies with her friends and would leave them after awhile and come up the stairs to the projection room during the course of the movie. She would leave just before the end of the movie in order to go home with her friends. This went on for three years! Eventually, in the eleventh grade, we were discovered! Her mother had come to the theater to find Missy and her friends couldn't answer to her whereabouts. Mrs. Rhodes asked at the front desk if they had seen her, and Laura Branch told her that Missy had gone up into the projection room.

Mrs. Rhodes came into the projection room and found us smooching behind the projector. Man, was I ever embarrassed! There was a brief confrontation that ended with Mrs. Rhodes taking Missy downstairs and out of the theater. It was two weeks later when Missy came to the projection room to see me and apologized for her mother's actions. She was now a "grown woman" (as she stated) and could see anyone she wanted. There would be no further confrontations, and now we could actually go out occasionally on dates.

Missy loved my VW about as much as I did. She began coming over on Sundays to help me care for the car and would even get a little dirty underneath it as she learned how to change the oil and filters. She had me at the word "Oil Change!" She became the first love of my life since I had never dated anyone else before. We dated each other up until graduation when she took a scholarship from the Daughters of the American Revolution to attend the University of Georgia. She wanted to become a pharmacist, so I dared not stand in her way by asking her to stay near Seymour. Oh, we stayed in touch through phone calls and letters, but things wouldn't be the same after that. College now had our attention and our relationship had drifted after a few months in our first year in college. Man, I really loved that girl! She loved me AND my VW, and that's one of the things which endeared me to this old car. I had thought of Missy many times over the past two years and wondered how things were going for her.

Chapter Three
The Road Home

My intentions were to graduate from Valdosta State with a degree in Sociology and work with either the prison system in Georgia or Juvenile Court Services. I had always wanted to help delinquents who were caught up in the system, and try to make a difference in the life of a teenager. I had a soft spot for those who couldn't help themselves. I had not realized the many difficult classes I would have to take, however, in order to achieve my goals. I guess anthropology was the worst one of all. I never could figure out how anthropology could help me to help others! I passed it by the hair of my chin!

There I was, pulling out of the parking lot at Abraham Baldwin College onto the main road on this sticky, very hot day in May. Blacktop asphalt. The heat was rising in plumes from the road ahead of me as I turned to the right at Johnson's Corner onto the back highway to Seymour. As I made my turn, this little old lady decided to cut me off, and I wound up on the edge of the road, steering hard to stay out of the ditch on the opposite side! Boy, was I fuming at her, but she had not missed a lick! She was already a mile down the road, unaware that she had almost cost me my life!

With my hands frozen to my steering wheel, I sat there on the roadside for the longest moment. It's like time standing still when you're caught in a situation like that. That was actually the closest call I've ever had and it startled me to the nth degree. I was shaking like a leaf on a limb on a very windy day! I had to calm my nerves before I could maneuver my VW back onto the highway.

As soon as my fear passed, I became very angry and asked how such a person could possibly get a driver's license. These people endanger our lives every single day, and they aren't even aware of it. Boy, would I love to have a few choice words with her right about now!

I headed north on State Highway 78 towards Seymour, much slower now than earlier, thanking God (under my breath) for saving me in that moment. I had regained my composure, for the most part, and turned on my radio, and the first song was one of my favorites, John Denver singing "Rocky Mountain High." That song always soothed me, and it brought a calmness that day in the midst of a near calamity. I loved music of all genre, but I had friends who couldn't stand to listen to the radio with me because of my broad choices. My friends only wanted to hear the popular rock songs of the day. I liked Mozart, Beethoven, Simon & Garfunkel, Aretha Franklin, Otis Redding from Macon, Georgia, and a host of other greats. I guess my favorite singer had to be John Denver. His songs were so melodic and smooth and reached into the heart. His songs always had a soothing effect on me. I had two of his 8-track tapes in my VW and both were already worn out! I knew every word to every song and had learned how to play them on my mother's flat-top guitar. I also had a fondness for Georgia Public Radio and how they presented the News Hour and other talk shows throughout the day. My friends didn't care for that kind of stuff on the radio either.

The highway loomed ahead of me now with only a few houses scattered along the way, mostly countryside, farm fields and a couple of dairies. It was a leisurely drive each day, and it gave me some quality time to reflect on my classes and to get my thoughts organized. I always felt completely comfortable alone behind the wheel of my best friend, my 1972 blue Volkswagen Super Beetle.

South Georgia is gorgeous in late spring, just before the killer temperatures of the summer come along. In late spring, fields are beginning to ripen with fresh corn, tomatoes, and other row crops. In the summers I always had the opportunity to visit my Uncle Roger and Aunt Myrtice Toombs down in Sparks, Georgia. Uncle Roger usually raised about 100 acres of watermelons and cantaloupes, and I would go down for a couple of weeks each summer and help him with the harvest. Working with many of the kids from neighboring farms, we would line up across the field and march from one end to the other picking the ripe melons and tossing them across the line to

the wagon where they were carefully stacked with a bit of
hay between them. At the end of the major harvest of melons, I would accompany Uncle Roger to the Atlanta
Farmer's Market. We would camp out at our assigned
booth day and night until the truck load of melons was
sold. I would meet kids from all over Georgia, Alabama,
South Carolina, and Tennessee who would come to the
Atlanta Market with relatives to sell fruit, row crops, or
whatever. We would play together and run around the
market with each other day and night. The adults would
sit and dip their snuff or chew their tobacco on the curbing
and talk about their crops or the woes that all farmers discuss whenever together. There's never enough rain, too
much humidity, seeds not germinating, labor too high to
hire enough workers to harvest, tractors and rigs breaking
down . . . Yet, it always amazed me that they lived in
really nice houses and drove around in Cadillacs while
their $150,000 harvesters sat rusting in the fields!

In retrospect, those days and nights at the Farmer's
Market in Atlanta were some of the best days of my life. I
learned a lot from other kids that I wasn't usually privy to
back home in Seymour. The older I became, the more I
learned during those hot summer days and nights. My first
kiss was from Carla Redden, a young twelve-year old
blonde from Sylvester, Georgia. It was crude and hastily
planted on me by Carla, but I remembered that kiss for
years. The sweet taste of watermelon wine was discovered
behind Fred's Restaurant there on the grounds of the

Farmer's Market. It came from a young boy (can't remember his name now) who lived in Cartersville, just a few miles from Atlanta. He had brought it from home and had shared a swig of it with me that night. The taste lingers with me to this day!

I always picked up extra cash at the market helping truckers load their trucks with the goods they had purchased. I remember one night that Uncle Roger allowed me to work from about 6 PM until 4 AM in the back of one of those long beds, stacking watermelons one on top of the other all the way to the top of the truck! Man, was I one tired puppy the next morning, but that $20 bill was worth it all. I could see ten movies back in Seymour with that $20 or buy me all the candy or ice cream I wanted at the local drugstore. Those were really sweet memories that are implanted in one's consciousness throughout life.

The kudzu was running wild along the tree-tops on Highway 78 and sapping the very breath out of everything it touched. Flowers were abundant in the woods and the dogwood trees still had a semblance of their flowers here and there, but were mostly gone.

It was a pleasant afternoon drive until that old lady pulled out in front of me and nearly took my life. I had found my composure, however, and John Denver rocked me on towards Seymour. Little did I realize that in a few moments of time, everything in my cozy little life would change forever. A harbinger of fate loomed ahead.

Chapter Four
Confrontation on the Hillside

There is a certain rhythm to every person's life. It may be composed of trills, staccatos, crescendos, but, indeed, a rhythm. What life holds in store for us may be conducted by the Master's hand with skillful and pre-determined meter, yet, may also be composed by the sheer hands of fate. A run-away rhythm may implode all plans or sequences and lead the spectator or recipient in the lurch. That which is constant, smooth, deliberate and di-rect, which holds together the meaning of our lives is the arpeggio. It rises and falls, yet always returns to its core root. The syncopation of life is filled with all the acciden-tals, the majors, the minors, augmented and diminished elements which comprise our existence. From this exis-tence, there is a certain rhythm. Though we may not like the outcome, we must play out this symphony of parts, looking ahead through a glass, darkly. To know the full score would be to our detriment, privy to the unrehearsed finale.

All that remains seem to be the skid marks of our

lives left behind as a trail or story of our finiteness; each representing a life, a person, an entity that once existed in space and time. Every skid mark tells a story. Our highways are marred with them. Long, short, black streaks across the road that symbolize something out of the ordinary which happened there. You can often find a roadside cross planted near the skid marks on our highways where family members or friends have marked the place of some tragedy, some death, some terrible incident that occurred. It gives one an uneasy feeling when passing by those marks, and are left to wonder what happened.

Picture a young teenager, or several perhaps, off on a joyous night of partying with friends. They buy a case of beer and begin their journey of a lifetime. The driver becomes a little disoriented and, BANG! off the edge of the road he goes! Unable to compensate for his state of drunkenness, he swerves back and forth onto the road too quickly and goes into a tail-spin. The car winds up jumping the ditch and slamming into a large tree. Skid marks follow the trail of the car's journey to doom. Someone's baby (now a teenager) sitting in the back seat is thrust rapidly across the front seat and through the windshield, killing him instantly! Another teenager, a young fifteen-year old girl, is crushed on the passenger side of the front seat as the car collapses on her side. Bright lights, sirens wailing in the dark of night, policemen and patrolmen everywhere as the ambulances carry off the remains of the night. Somewhere, in just a short while, families will be notified that their precious children will not be coming home. Funeral plans are made. An entire community mourns its loss. Such precious lives, filled with potential, cut down in a moment's frenzy, and comes to a close.

Consider another scenario. A young mother of two is driving home after a Tupperware party at a friend's home. On a long stretch of blacktop, late at night, she en-counters a deer crossing the road. BANG! The deer hits the front bumper, sending her car into a tail-spin. She ends the journey upside down in the ditch with a broken neck. Not another scratch on her body, yet she is dead. The skid marks tell the eerie story of that fateful night. Her husband and children visit that roadside frequently and have set up a shrine there in her memory. A cross is placed near the spot of her death, and flowers are brought on her birthday, their anniversary, and at other special occasions. What a sad legend for the couple of marks on the highway!

I had never really been one to believe much in mere fate. I had always figured that a person was in charge of his or her own life and could change the out-come of it by making wise decisions along the way. I've always been a big Robert Frost fan and remember receiv-ing high honors from my eleventh grade teacher, Clara Dumas, for my comments on the Frost poem entitled *"The Road Not Taken."* My favorite line was:

"...somewhere ages and ages hence; two
roads diverged in a wood,
and I—I took the one less traveled by, and
that has made all the difference."

You see, I've always felt that our decisions at every turn in the road dictate for us the final outcome. If a person wanted to go to college and didn't have the means, there is always a way around that. If one really wanted to do something desired, it was always possible, merely by the choices made. I believed in that philosophy and lived by it.

Halfway home to Seymour that afternoon, I began to feel a bit sleepy and had to keep slapping my face to stay awake. I guess I would learn to get more sleep the night before an exam! At any rate, the sun was glaring into the windshield on my old blue VW. I had my left arm propped up on the driver's side window and was enjoying the warm breeze as it blew into the car across my face. I had pulled off the road and had tried to awaken myself to a more conscious state at one point, and then it was back to the task of driving home. I had traveled this stretch of highway for the past two years and could almost drive it blindfolded.

I had not passed a single car in either direction now for the past ten minutes. It seemed a bit unusual to me, especially for a Friday. I often took this back way home because it was faster and I could really turn up the speed a little more than I could over on State Road 92.

Besides, the Georgia State Patrol always monitored 92
more than 78. The patrolmen were like vultures waiting
on speeding college students, ready to pounce on them at
a moment's notice. They backed up into little trails and
roads off the side of the highway and just sat there and
waited on their next victims. I had already received one
warning ticket last year on Highway 92, so I had decided
then to take this route home more often.

Twenty one miles from Tifton, toward Seymour,
Highway 78 came to an end. That is where you pick up
Highway 92 again. A simple stop sign marked the ending
of 78. From that point on to Seymour, I would really have
to watch my speed because of the lurking vultures. The
Cataluchie River crossing was approximately 500 yards
up 92 towards Seymour from the stop sign. It was a large
concrete span over the river swamp and murky waters of
the Cataluchie. On both sides of the bridge one could see
the swampy areas with its marsh and wildlife, usually a
blue heron or two stalking their prey, some occasional
wood ducks floating around and, if you were lucky, possibly a red fox or deer passing through the swamp. The
bridge and river were several miles from any habitation.
Large holes had been dug out from the sand beds on either
side of the river. Folks came here for the sand to mix mor-
tar with, or to use as landfill, etc. Just up the road from the
river, straight as an arrow from the bridge, was a very
steep hill. At the top of the hill, the road turned sharply
downward and off to the right. It was a no-passing zone

and had always been a terrible spot for passing motorists. Several wrecks had taken place on that curve and hilltop in the past, and I always slowed down while climbing the hill, unable to see what could be approaching from the other side.

Everything from that point on became a blur as I sat momentarily at the stop sign. I gazed up 92 across the river bridge and something caught my eye. At first, I couldn't figure out what it was, being over a half-mile away from my vantage point. I strained my eyes to try and make it out. Smoke was billowing up from the top of the hill and two large objects were apparently strewn across the highway. My first thoughts were that two cars had collided on Crookman's Hill. "Oh, my God!" I thought.

Crookman's Hill was so named because Homer Crook was a long-time resident of Seymour and had the first major wreck there on the hill and had died as a result not long after the State of Georgia paved the old dirt road that once existed. That was long before my time, but folks still called it Crookman's Hill.

Crookman's Hill would become my nemesis.

Chapter Five
Miss Anna Louise Miller

"Anna Louise Miller, hurry up, girl, if you're going to school with us today!" It was her mother's voice calling as usual from the front porch. Of course, Anna Louise had to be properly attired, for she was a proper young lady, full of life and from a good family of the south. Today, she hoped, would be a very special day for her. She would discover that night at Henderson Stadium whether or not she had been elected by her Senior Class as this year's Homecoming Queen! She felt that it would either be herself or her best friend, Melody Harper (although it was her heartfelt desire to win). She would be content, however, if the class chose Melody, just a bit heartbroken. The two had shared their first sixteen years together, living only two blocks apart, and beginning first grade together. They had been closer than sisters through the years and had shared all things in common. In fact, Mrs. Miller would stop around the corner and pick Melody up for school each day on their way in. It had always been that way. Fairaday, Georgia, was a small town of approximately 2,400 people. The main attraction on Friday nights was the local high school football game. Everyone came out for the game to support their beloved hometown Cavaliers. Anna Louise hoped that either she or Melody would walk out to the fifty-yard line during the halftime show and one would be crowned Homecoming Queen and the other as Runner-Up. What a tremendous honor, Anna Louise thought, to be chosen by one's peers.

"Stop drooling at that mirror and hurry up, child. We're going to be late," Mrs. Miller retorted. "Enough is enough, dear. We've got to get there earlier than usual this morning for I have to meet with Principal Jones about the new teacher." Mrs. Miller was the lead teacher for the fifth grade at Tompkins Elementary School, and was to meet today with Principal Jones to discuss the hiring of a new teacher to fill the vacancy left by Mrs. Peggy Sturdivant who had taken maternity leave a little sooner than expected.

"Alright, mom, I'm on my way. Just hold your tatters for another minute," Anna Louise replied, finishing up her lipstick and beholding her beauty one last time in the mirror. Jason, her younger twelve-year-old pest of a brother, yelled at her to come on when she suddenly appeared on the porch, ready to go. She really looked lovely, Mrs. Miller thought, and would be so disappointed tonight if she did not win Homecoming Queen. She had built her hopes so high that she would really be hurt if things went in the other direction and someone else was elected

Queen. Mrs. Miller had wondered how Anna Louise would take the disappointment. Yet, she knew that Anna Louise was quite the independent young lady and felt that she would be fine with whatever decision. She had a brilliant mind and excelled in basketball and cheerleading, and was a straight-A student in every subject. One could not ask for a better daughter! She even sang each Sunday in the Fairaday United Methodist Church choir and would provide the congregation with a solo anthem on occasion. She could really raise the roof with her renditions of "Ave Maria" or "I'll Fly Away" or other such numbers the congregation loved for her to sing. Murtice Tillman was the pianist at the church and was known to be able to accompany anyone and thoroughly enjoyed playing for Anna Louise. It was always interesting to see how the older folk sat listening to Anna Louise sing with her songbird voice as though they could listen to her all day!

The Millers stopped at the corner as usual and picked up Melody who was also very excited about the day. She was beaming from ear-to-ear with exuberance, and the glow on her face could be seen a block away as she entered the backseat of the Miller's car. Jason Miller always accompanied his mother in the front seat while Melody and Anna Louise talked girl-talk to and from school in the back. Jason couldn't stand to hear their conversations and always tried to keep the radio loud enough to drown out their girlish giggles and talk, but Mrs. Miller wouldn't allow him to turn it up too loud.

"Good morning, Millers!" Melody said, as she entered the car and took her place in the backseat. "What a wonderful, wonderful day for two very special girls!"

Jason could have croaked but held his tongue.

Mrs. Miller started up. "Melody, dear, I think that both of you have an equal chance of winning Homecoming Queen tonight, and you know how much I love the both of you, so I'm not going to make predictions. I will be more than happy if either of you wins." Mrs. Miller was a very dedicated and loving mother, but she realized that Melody was a very important part of their family as well. She had spent many long hours and days at the Miller home with Anna Louise and had gone with them on several of their vacations through the years.

Melody's family consisted only of her mother, Amanda Harper, who worked at the local pants factory in Fairaday as a seamstress. She had been there for over 20 years and was a very faithful and dedicated worker, always making production and staying ahead of the game. She had to quit school in the tenth grade because she had become pregnant with Melody. This had always been hush-hush involving any conversation about Melody or her family. The truth is that Owen Lambert from Ridgecrest had one date with Amanda Harper midway through the eighth grade. The results were devastating, but Amanda had been a good mother and loved Melody dearly with all of her heart. Owen was drafted before the baby came and was sent to Vietnam and was killed in action just outside Saigon while on patrol with a group of his fellow soldiers. Amanda had tried her best to raise Melody in a good God-fearing home with all of her immediate needs being met. She and Melody had continued to live in her mother's home. Sally Harper had died when Amanda was eight months pregnant with Melody. She had been fighting Leukemia for six years and had finally lost the battle. Cyrus Harper, Amanda's father, had died in a tragic farming accident when his right arm had been caught in the wheels of a combine. He had been trying to clean out the trash that had accumulated in the combine so that it would turn again freely. At the same moment, his arm was engaged and he couldn't loosen it from the wheels. The coroner said that he had been in that situation from around 10 AM in the morning until late that afternoon when Frank Barton had come to check on him. Frank owned the farm that Cyrus was sharecropping at the time. Cyrus had simply bled to death.

Amanda Harper had to be at work at the factory each morning at 7 AM, so the driving schedule with the Millers had worked out great for years. The Millers did not mind at all since the two girls were so close. It had become a daily routine for all involved and meant a lot to Mrs. Harper for the Millers to take care of Melody.

Jason reached over the seat, patted Melody on the head as she entered the car and then said, "Melody, you've got my vote for Homecoming Queen! When are we going out on our first date together? Huh?"

"Jason!" Mrs. Miller shouted, "What are you trying to do to your sister? Don't you realize that you've just hurt her feelings? Now you apologize right this second to her or you won't even be going to the game tonight!" Mrs. Miller was beside herself.

"That's O.K. mom," Anna Louise responded. "It's his choice. I voted for Melody as well, and I think that she would make an excellent Queen." With that, Melody reached over and took Anna Louise's hand in hers and both let out one of those despicable girlish screams of joy! Jason cringed in the front seat!

Mrs. Miller accepted Anna Louise's response, but she reprimanded Jason for his smart remarks in the presence of his sister. His attitude lately had gotten him into a lot of trouble with Mrs. Miller. Mrs. Fryer, Jason's homeroom teacher, had caught him shooting spit-balls a couple of weeks back and had written him up, sending him to the office. When his mom heard of it that night, being the teacher she was, Jason received one week of yard work, dish-washing, no TV, no radio, and numerous little math problems that his mom had dreamed up for him to do! His life was completely miserable that week and he had promised never to shoot another spit-ball at anyone. Truth is that Jason had hit Mrs. Fryer with one of his shots, and this had really angered his mom! The little brat was always doing something devilish, and so Anna Louise and Melody took him at face-value most of the time.

The Rev. John Henry Miller, Anna Louise's father, was pastor at the Fairaday United Methodist Church, a pastorate he had successfully held now for the past fifteen years, actually unheard of in most Methodist circles! Most ministers serve for an average of four years and are then reappointed to another parish.

The Fairaday United Methodist Church was a
moderate sized county seat church that had provided a
broader family for the Miller's during these years. Rev.
Miller was a very popular man about town who served on
practically every board and commission of the city and
county. People dearly loved the Millers, and even the
Baptists came to their church when something special was
taking place. He had performed many funeral services for
both Baptists and Methodists in Fairaday during his fifteen year run, and the Baptists would often call upon him
for counseling, marriages, and funeral services when they
would be in between pastors. He had always gladly
obliged them. He was truly a revered minister to all folks
in the surrounding area.

John Henry Miller had known from Day One that
his daughter Anna Louise was blessed by God as a special
person. He had watched her grow and mature into a beautiful and vibrant young lady, full of grace and poise. Her
witness and testimony had been shared among the folks in
Fairaday many times in the past, and folks still wanted to
hear it again and again. It's an amazing story of faith and
endurance that set her apart in the community.

Anna Louise had been born with leukemia and had
to undergo numerous treatments through the years. She
was sent to Egelston Children's Hospital at Emory University in Atlanta each time she needed treatments. She

had been in remission for the past eight years, and there were no signs of any reoccurrence of the cancer. People had prayed this young girl through these difficult years and felt as though they personally had some part in her recovery process. Indeed, they did have, through their wonderful support of the family. Fundraisers for Anna Louise had been ample among the folks in Fairaday and Collier County in order to help the family with their medical expenses. This little vibrant girl had helped to pull various factions in the county together over the one issue of her illness. She was their bright and shining light, and everyone loved her.

The Miller family truly felt blessed by God. Yet, they knew that things could suddenly change at a moment's notice, and Anna Louise could have a reoccurrence of the cancer. Their prayer lives were deeply entrenched, to say the least! She was on every prayer list at churches in the county and even beyond. People would call the Methodist parsonage to check on her, some from as far away as Macon. The Millers had seen the hands of God at work through the many caring and concerned people in their lives.

Mrs. Miller dropped the girls off at the high school and then rounded the corner and dropped Jason off in front of the middle school. Jason said a final word to his mom before heading into school. "Mom, I apologize for what I said in the car about Melody, and please forgive me for my little visit to the Principal's office two weeks ago. You also should know that I am 150% percent behind my sister as Homecoming Queen. I was just trying to get them started, you know!"

"I understand, sweetie, but watch it from now on. You are riding on a very thin rail with both me and your father at the present, so be careful what you do and say. Did you finish your math homework?" Mrs. Miller inquired.

"Yes, mother. Dad helped me with it last night. It was a lot easier than I thought it would be. Thanks for asking, though." And with that, Mrs. Miller made her appointment in time at Tompkins Elementary.

That evening, the Millers loaded up their Suburban and headed for Fairaday High School where the Cavaliers were to face the Raiders from Simpson High in this Homecoming Battle. It was always a tough battle between these two neighboring schools, and tonight it would be no different. The little stadium would only hold a maximum of 1,000 people on both sides combined, so a lot of folk would have to stand at either end of the stadium (near the hedges). This game usually brought in about 1,200 to 1,500 people from both counties. Quite a lot, considering how small both counties were.

Mrs. Miller queried her husband John Henry as they exited the Suburban in the high school parking lot with Jason tagging along behind. "Honey, did everything go O.K. when you took Anna Louise this afternoon for her dress rehearsal?"

"Sure did, Hon. She was so excited that I think she was actually walking on air as she entered the gymnasium," replied John. "I don't think I've ever seen her happier, dear. There was a certain aura about her, which illuminated everything in the gym. Only hitch was that we had forgotten her shoes back at home, and I had to make a quick return trip to fetch them for her. Guess that's why she was literally 'walking on air'!"

"Did she have everything she needed then?" Mrs. Miller asked, implying that she had been unable to come home in time to get everything ready for Anna Louise.

"Honey, it has all been taken care of! Don't fret yourself. She'll be fine tonight. Remember, that little girl has everything taken care of, I assure you. You know how independent she is," Rev. Miller said.

"I know, John, but I still worry about her. Did she take her medication like I asked her to?" Mrs. Miller was the family worry-wort. She was always the one taking care of every tiny detail of her family's life and would not rest easy until this evening was over. Her three hours in the stands tonight would be grueling for her.

"Yes, dear, I personally watched her take the medicine in the kitchen just before we left. All is firmly under control. Just relax now and enjoy yourself for a change. Forget about school, forget about teaching . . . and just be a mother and wife tonight. Anna Louise needs us now more than ever." John's voice almost cracked as he finished his statement. He realized that a miracle was taking place before their very eyes. This young blessing from God was now sweet-sixteen and in the Homecoming Contest for Queen of her high school. Who could possibly have thought that this day would ever arrive sixteen years ago? They had prayed as a family and as a community night and day for the first few weeks of her life. Anna Louise was only 3-1/2 pounds at birth, having arrived a month earlier than predicted. Margie had many difficulties during the pregnancy and had fought tooth and nail the last few weeks prior to her birth to endure the pain. The last two weeks of the pregnancy were spent in bed— doctor's orders!

At one-year old, doctors at Egleston Hospital in Atlanta had discovered the leukemia. Now little Anna Louise Miller seemed to have two strikes against her. The doctors had sat the Millers down and had gone into detailed discussions with them that they would be extremely lucky people if Anna Louise saw her fifth birthday! Yet, miraculously, she had been quite the little fighter, and had grown, bit-by-bit, to the place where she was tonight. The Millers had seen and experienced a lot through the years: hospitals in Florida and Georgia, many specialists, bone-marrow transplants, blood transfusions, narrow escapes from the jaws of death, Anna Louise's several bouts with pneumonia, and the inescapable bad times emotionally and physically for Anna Louise. It literally broke their hearts to see their sweet little girl go through such terrible treatments, but she was always the little trooper. That's exactly what endeared her to so many people and had won their hearts. In a sense, Rev. John Henry Miller thought it would be a fitting tribute from her school friends for Anna Louise to be selected tonight as Homecoming Queen. It was, at this point, in the hands of fate.

Chapter Six
Half Time

The game between Fairaday and Simpson was electric in every way. An early evening shower had made the playing field sloppy from the start. Fairaday had scored first, on a fumble recovery during the kick-off, from the six-yard-line. Roddy Pace, fullback for Fairaday, scored the first points of the game when he leap-frogged over the line on the very first play from scrimmage. FAIRADAY – 06, SIMPSON – 00. James Suttle, our place kicker, missed the extra point and landed on his back. The ground was so saturated with water that he had slipped in the process of kicking. It took the longest period of time for the coaches and the local E.M.T. to check out James who went down hard on his back. After about ten minutes, they placed him on a stretcher and carted him off to the locker room from which they later transported him to the hospital over in Jasper. He had been knocked unconscious from the blow to his back. We later discovered that evening that he would be fine, just really shaken up.

Back and forth, back and forth the game went in the first half. The Simpson Cavaliers finally scored on a long pass play down the sidelines from midfield. Their extra point attempt was good, so Simpson led all the way from the middle of the first quarter until the half, SIMPSON – 07, FAIRADAY – 06. The late evening mist was forming everywhere now following the afternoon shower. The field was hard to see from the stands. The Millers had a difficult time trying to figure out who had the ball at any given time. They could only sit there and see the bright red glow of the scoreboard at the south end of the stadium to discern who was ahead.

Rev. Miller was very proud of that scoreboard, for he had been instrumental in getting Reiger Electric Company to purchase it for the school two years ago. Rev. Miller was always involved in some community project or fundraiser for the citizens of Fairaday or Collier County. He was a good man and a concerned citizen.

Amanda Harper came in just before half time because she had been unable to get off work at her usual time. The pants factory was behind in their quotas, and so they had asked everyone to work late. Amanda had begged her supervisor to let her off early to be with her daughter at the stadium, but to little avail. She was allowed to leave at 8:00 PM, however, and made a mad beeline to the stadium. She was out of breath when she walked up the bleachers to where the Millers sat. The Millers had always purchased season tickets for themselves as well as the Harpers for several years. Rev. Miller was co-chair of the Booster Club and was given the opportunity several times for better seats closer to the field, but he had always accepted their first assigned seats, twenty rows up and near the 30 yard line in the reserved section. He was an humble man and wouldn't dare take someone else's seats. That wouldn't be proper to him.

"Amanda," Margie Miller called when she saw her coming up the bleachers, "Where on God's green earth have you been?"

"Oh, it's that supervisor of mine at the plant. He wouldn't let us go early even with me telling him how important this night was. He was really being cruel to all of us. He knew it was Homecoming, but he had no sympathy for us at all." One could hear the anger in Amanda's voice. "Looking at the scoreboard, seems like it's been a very close one," Amanda stated.

"Yes it has, Amanda," Rev. Miller answered. "Messy, messy game. We've been having a hard time just seeing the players on the field. Can't imagine what it's going to be like walking out there during the Homecoming processional. I do hope that you guys can see what's going on. I just feel so bad that the night had to turn out so misty."

"Well, Brother John, seems that a lot of things haven't gone our way tonight!" Amanda Harper replied. "But everything will turn out fine, I'm sure. I have confidence that the half time show will be just great and our little girls will be so proud to walk out on that field with the rest of the court." One could sense a nervousness in Amanda's reply. The mad rush she had just been through from the factory to the field, the long day behind the sewing machine, the demand to make production all day—and now less than perfect weather when her little girl was to have her moment of glory! Life doesn't seem fair at times such as these.

"God bless you, Amanda," Rev. Miller said, as he took his towel and wiped out her seat next to Margie Miller. The Millers always sat with the Dopson couple from their church on one side and Melody and Amanda Harper on the other. "I am so sorry that you have had to endure such cruel treatment on such a special night. Things shouldn't have to be that way, but we take our punches as we go, I guess."

Rev. Miller asked Amanda if she was excited for Melody, and she responded: "Brother John, now you know that I'm pulling for BOTH of our little girls! Why would you ask me such a question? You know I'll be completely happy if either one of them wins. I just want them both to be happy."

Reverend Miller agreed with Amanda and patted her hands, realizing the many pairs of pants she had probably stitched that day alone at the factory. Amanda was a choir member at the Methodist Church and also served as one of the Communion Stewards. She was a very faithful lady, and nothing ever seemed to rattle her, but Reverend Miller had sensed a bit of frustration in her voice over her situation at work. Amanda had done a great job raising Melody alone as a single mom. It was a difficult job, but the two of them seemed to work so well together, almost like sisters. Amanda had, no doubt, made many sacrifices for Melody over the years to see to it that Melody had every possible opportunity to succeed in life. Amanda was from a very poor background, but she had managed to raise her beautiful and very talented daughter in a secure home.

Just before half time, Simpson scored another touchdown making it 14-06 in their favor. You could hear a pin drop on the Fairaday side of the field. Everyone seemed really disappointed in their team's efforts at this point. Fairaday almost scored from the three yard line as the buzzer sounded the end of the half. Our half back ran around the right end with the ball and fell just inches short of the goal line. A great big "Ohhhh!" came from the Fairaday crowd as the buzzer broke through the misty night. It was a symbol of everyone's disappointment.

The two teams then retreated to their respective locker rooms in the gymnasium, except for the players who would be chaperones for the candidates for Homecoming Queen. Brad Peterson, Anna Louise's chaperone and team quarterback, would come over to the sidelines where all the candidates and chaperones would gather. Brad had been Anna Louise's boyfriend since elementary school and was a fantastic young man in every respect. He was well disciplined and a hard worker. He had lettered all four years in high school baseball, basketball and football, an almost unbelievable feat for any high school student. All of this and he still made the honor roll each semester! He was the son of Joe and Carol Peterson of Fairaday. Joe was president at the Bank of Fairaday, and he and his family were very faithful Baptists at First Baptist Church, a congregation located two blocks from the Fairaday United Methodist Church.

Brad was an avid hunter and would bring in at least an 8 or 10 point buck each season. He and his father would dress-out each deer and grind the meat into hamburger meat, meatloaf, or even steaks for freezing. Their freezer stayed full of deer meat year-round. They would often share it with the Millers and with Amanda and her daughter Melody. Brad and his father had three quarter horses and maintained a 50 acre hay field to keep their horses and 10 head of cattle fed. Deep woods surrounded the remaining 250 acres of their spread. It was a beautiful place and was well admired by passersby. This had been the family farm for well over 150 years.

The Simpson band began marching onto the field and did two numbers before the Fairaday band was to perform. Fairaday marched out to midfield with enthusiasm and did a beautiful rendition of "God Bless America!" Following the song, the loud speaker announcer, Patrick Swain from the Post Office, began the Homecoming procedures.

"Ladies and Gentlemen, tonight, six lovely young ladies are competing for Fairaday High School Homecoming Queen. All are winners to us, but only one will be chosen from votes received by their student body. This process culminates tonight in the crowning of our new Queen. Here to present our new Queen with her crown is the lovely Miss Vickie Morant, last year's reigning Queen." Patrick Swain's voice was blaring across the stadium and filtering through the pine trees beyond the high school campus. It seemed to reverberate in the sudden chill of the night and through the mist, which continued to float around the stadium.

Patrick Swain then began the introductions of the six candidates and their chaperones. "At the fifty yard line, we have the lovely Alice Jones and her chaperone, Warren Bird. Alice is the daughter of Henry and Renee Jones and is a varsity cheerleader and co-president of her senior class. Let's hear it for Alice Jones!" Mr. Swain's voice rose in tempo at the end, as the crowd on both sides of the field cheered. Alice was attired in a blue sequined v-neck gown.

Mr. Swain paused as the couple walked to the center of the field, just in front of the band which was lined up across the field from end zone to end zone. Alice was a beautiful redhead and a close friend of the other five candidates. She and Anna Louise had taken piano lessons together for six years from old lady Mumford down on Hall Street in Fairaday. Old lady Mumford was a stern and stubborn old soul, an old maid, and had served in the Navy as a Wave for six years during World War II. Folks around Fairaday knew her abilities on the piano and those who could afford her fees would have their children take lessons from her. Alice and Anna Louise stopped taking lessons when their interest in cheerleading took center stage three years ago.

"Next, we have the radiant Miss Amber Spoon. Amber is being escorted by Ron Fletcher. Amber is the daughter of Eveleen Cooper and the late Peter Cooper. Amber maintains a 3.8 grade point average and is a junior this year at Fairaday High. She is a member of the Glee Club, the Debate Team, and has played on the High School basketball team as a guard for the past three years. Let's hear it for Amber Spoon!" Mr. Swain's voice grew louder and louder with each announcement. Amber was dressed in a pink gown adorned with beautiful white pearls.

Amber had been in a tragic wreck in the ninth grade with three other students out at Horse Pen Corners. It was a four-way stop out in the middle of nowhere. Two roads crossed, and the intersection had always been a dangerous spot for travelers. Amber and her three friends, Sylvia Curtis, Tom Brandy, and Elizabeth Sparks, were on their way back home from a football game. Tom Brandy was driving his father's Buick. Tom, who was a couple of years older than Amber and Sylvia, had dated Elizabeth Sparks for two years. Elizabeth and Tom were both in the eleventh grade and had offered to carry Amber and Sylvia with them that night.

They had reached Horse Pen Corners near midnight. Tom had come to a stop at the sign, when all of a sudden a red pickup truck came barreling out from nowhere. It was swerving out of control, crossing back and forth on the blacktop road in front of the four as they sat watching it. It happened so quickly that Tom did not have a chance to back up or move the Buick before the pickup truck struck them on the passenger side where Elizabeth was sitting. The carnage afterwards was awful. Elizabeth was crushed immediately upon impact, and Tom was knocked unconscious with six broken ribs and lacerations about the face and upper torso. Sylvia wound up with bruises and a broken collarbone and three days in the local hospital, but Amber, who had escaped unharmed, was really torn apart inside! She was a nervous wreck for weeks after the incident and had to miss school for two weeks for daily counseling in order to regain her sanity.

The community of Fairaday mourned for days the death of Elizabeth. She had been such a bright and promising citizen and a model high school student. She was a leader in various areas and was a great debator on the debate team with Amber. That night, and the events of it, would haunt the kids of Fairaday High School for years to come! Kids driving out that way would always respect Horse Pen Corners. Her friends erected a cross with the simple name 'Elizabeth' engraved upon it, on the roadside. It was visited frequently by students and friends for years.

David Flanders and Terry Foster were the two teenagers in the pickup truck. They were returning home to Burns Creek from a night on the town. They had secured a couple of six-packs at the liquor store out on the Coolidge County line before leaving their home area and had been driving through the night around Fairaday looking for girls. It was an old tradition in that area that boys from one neighboring county would venture (at risk) across county lines to try and pick up girls in the other county. Sometimes they were successful but were never welcomed by the Fairaday boys.

David Flanders was driving his father's pickup and had had his drivers license for about six months. He was a cocky individual, and he and his friend Terry were self-proclaimed 'Red Necks.'

With their heads swimming around with a blood alcohol content, they were both impervious to the night. David was putting the pedal-to-the metal without any regards to the road conditions or how fast he was going. The Georgia State Patrol stated later, following their investigation, that the kid had to be driving in excess of 90 miles an hour upon impact with the Buick. Both boys survived miraculously. David Flanders had a concussion and two broken ribs while Terry Foster had minor lacerations about the face and arms. The pickup and the Buick were both totaled in the crash. Both boys were taken into Fairaday

and treated at the local clinic and then carried to the Fairaday jail where they remained until their Juvenile Court
hearing three weeks later. Both boys received one-year of
probation and community service. Such a small price to
pay for such a beautiful life as that of Elizabeth Sparks,
not to mention the other injuries and the wrecked lives
their frivolity had caused!

"And now, may I introduce to you Miss Melody
Harper, lovely daughter of Mrs. Amanda Harper. Melody
is being escorted by Glenn Jones. Melody has lettered four
years on the High School Cheerleading Squad and Basketball team. She excels in her studies and has maintained a
great 3.9 grade point average. Ladies and Gentlemen,
Miss Melody Harper!" Patrick Swain's voice maintained
a certain air about it. The crowd was exuberant as Melody
and Glenn made their way to the center of the field and
took their positions, continuing to hold arms while facing
the home crowd. Amanda Harper's heart was about to
burst as she looked out on her precious and dear little girl
and thought back suddenly through the years of their
struggles just to make ends meet and how good Melody
was in helping her mom with everything. She deserves
this special moment in her life, Amanda thought to herself
as she gazed out at Melody. It had been a long but special
journey for the both of them, and their respect and love for
each other was apparent. Melody wore a lovely blue sequined dress, which Amanda purchased in Macon while
on one of their recent visits there with her brother and

wife. It had cost her an entire week's wages at the Pants Factory, but Amanda felt that this was such a special time for Melody that it warranted the spending.

Mr. Swain's voice trilled in once again. "Ladies and Gentlemen, let me now introduce you to the vibrant and vivacious Carla Sikes! Carla is the daughter of Wilbur and Joan Sikes of Twin Corners (a neighborhood a few miles out on Rural Route 4). Carla is being escorted by Noel Webb. Carla is a member of the Beta Club, Tri-Hi-Y, the Better Homemaker's Club, and Guys and Dolls Drama Team. She maintains a 3.5 grade point average. Let's hear it for Miss Carla Sikes!" Carla was wearing a long white gown, nicely appointed with sequins down both sides and across the bodice.

For Reverend and Mrs. John Henry Miller, the hands of time seemed to completely stop! Their hearts were pounding inside their chests. The suspense was killing them both, and it was hard to catch their breaths. The anticipation was heavy. Knowing that their daughter, Anna Louise, would be called last to march to the center of the field had finally come with Mr. Swain's announcement.

"And now, our last candidate for Homecoming Queen. Ladies and Gentlemen, the beautiful Miss Anna Louise Miller, daughter of the Reverend and Mrs. John Henry Miller. She is being escorted tonight by Brad Peterson . . ." Before Mr. Swain could get another word in, the home crowd went berserk! They were all screaming and yelling uncontrollably! Reverend Miller felt a tightness in his chest and only prayed it wasn't a heart attack! He was so awed by the response of the crowd of people but knew exactly what she had meant to this entire community through the years.

After an eternity, Mr. Swain was able to continue. "Anna Louise has lettered four straight years as a guard on our basketball team and as a cheerleader on the cheerleading squad. She has excelled in all of her studies and has maintained a perfect 4.0 grade point average. Let's hear it again for Miss Anna Louise Miller!" Again, the crowd went crazy, and it pleased Margie Miller. Margie looked over at Jason, and he had tears streaming down his cheeks for his sister. Margie looked beyond Jason to Amanda Harper, and they both moved towards each other and embraced for the longest moment. Anna Louise was wearing a beautiful green chiffon gown that seemed to glow across the stadium and was highlighted by the bright lights glaring from above.

Brad Peterson, Anna Louise's escort and boyfriend, gripped tightly to her hand as he held it. He looked at her repeatedly, with the biggest smile on his face, for he knew how special and dear she was to him. How could this small framed little angel make such a tremendous impact on an entire community as she had? It was amazing to Brad and everyone else in the stadium that night.

Anna Louise Miller was beside herself! Tears streamed from her eyes as she watched and listened to the noisy crowd of people cheering her on. She wondered what she had done so special to warrant such a ranting. She would never really know. Brad was standing there beside her in his football uniform, Number 16, and she felt like the world was in the palm of her hands at that moment in time.

Reverend John Henry Miller could see Anna Louise's face glow down on the field, even through the misty fog now encroaching. There was a complete aura about her and he wondered if others could see it. Anna Louise was so excited that her father knew the butterflies had to be churning inside, for they were certainly churning within his being!

After all the candidates had been introduced and had taken their places on the field, Mr. Swain started again on the P.A. system. "Our second-runner-up tonight is the lovely Miss Amber Spoon. Congratulations, Miss Spoon. Your peers have spoken!"

After Vickie Morant placed the shash for second runner up around Amber's shoulder and neck, Mr. Swain continued. "Our first-runner-up for this year's Homecoming Queen is . . ." Silence fell upon the stadium crowd. Both sides were awaiting the response which seemed an eternity to Amanda Harper and the Miller Family. What a situation! Both Anna Louise and Melody Harper were well qualified, well admired, and loved by the student body. Both were very special individuals and deserving of the honor, but only one of the two would be chosen as the

1965 Fairaday High School Homecoming Queen. The moment of truth was now before them.

Mr. Swain's voice finished the sentence: "Our first-runner-up for this year's Homecoming Queen is Miss Melody Harper! Let's hear it for Melody. The crowd again cheered for Melody, as before, while Vickie Morant placed the first runner up shash over her shoulder. Melody was now praying that Anna Louise would be chosen as Queen. There were three other very notable candidates in the court, so it wasn't a given that Anna Louise would be Queen. Tension could be cut with a knife! Everyone in the stadium froze in a moment of time as Mr. Swain's voice continued.

"And now, ladies and gentlemen, it is with distinct honor and privilege that I announce to you the winner of this year's Homecoming Queen. It is the beautiful, the lovely, the talented ANNA LOUISE MILLER! Let's hear it, crowd, for Anna Louise." Mr. Swain's voice finally cracked as he made the announcement. He had known Anna Louise since birth and had watched her progress through all of her illnesses, hospitalizations and changes to where she was now. Finally, Mr. Swain could not hold back his tears.

All of the candidates came over with their escorts to congratulate and to hug Anna Louise at the midfield stripe. Vickie Morant placed the beautiful crown on her head, pinning it securely under her hair with bobbie-pins. Anna almost collapsed from all of the excitement and the finality of it all. Her brother Jason came running down the bleachers and onto the field to where Anna Louise was and hugged her. He then began jumping up and down like a nut. Anna Louise was a bit embarrassed but allowed him to do his thing, after all, her brother was happy for her. He then turned and hugged Melody as well.

Call it fate if you will, but all odds pointed this night to the one person who seemed to be in the spotlight on this occasion: ANNA LOUISE MILLER. When her name was finally announced, the football game had been forgotten. Time had frozen in place, and nothing else seemed to matter in Fairaday, Georgia, at that point. ANNA LOUISE MILLER – HOMECOMING QUEEN, 1965! Those would be the exact headlines in the Fairaday Sentinel the following week. There wasn't a dry-eye in that stadium on that misty cool evening when fate had spoken once again.

As soon as the band and the entourage had left the field, the football players returned to their sidelines from their respective locker rooms. Brad Peterson had a game of his own to play now, and a catch-up game at that. Fairaday was behind 14-06 and would receive the kick-off in the second half. Brad would lead the team down to the 14 yard line and then fail on fourth down and inches. Since James Suttle was out of the game, no one else on the team could try for a field goal, and so the team had run another play in an attempt at a first down. The ball then reverted back to Simpson High. They went straight down the field in 3:25 seconds and scored a touchdown on a 10 yard pass from the quarterback to their tight end. SIMP-SON 21- FAIRADAY 06. The game had taken a definite turn for the worse. The Fairaday crowd was dejected. Even the cheerleaders couldn't muster up a response.

Upon the ensuing kickoff to Fairaday, little Bob Curtis took the catch and went 92 yards down the right sideline and scored a quick 6 points. The Fairaday crowd now had new life. Brad Peterson took the ball on the next play and ran around the right side and sneaked in between several defenders for the two-point conversion. The score now was SIMPSON 21 – FAIRADAY 14. The third quarter ended as Simpson fumbled the ball on the 50 yard line and John Hayden, defensive back for Fairaday, fell on it.

Fourth quarter began with a wet field, a fog rolling in, and Simpson a touchdown behind. Something seemed electric in the air. The crowd for Faraday was anxious. Could they pull this thing back even again? Suddenly, on second down and 15, following a penalty for off-sides, Roddy Pace, the big fullback for Fairaday, took the hand-off from Brad Peterson on the 40 yard line and somehow found a seam between two defenders, scampering down the middle of the field untouched! SIMPSON 21 – FAIRADAY 20. What to do again about the extra point! Brad called a play for the right half back to veer off center and dive. The play was successful and Fairaday finally had the lead: FAIRADAY 22 – SIMPSON 21. The crowd was electric again!

There were two more possessions for each team with the clock winding down in the fourth quarter. Simpson came close both times, but came away with nothing, missing two field goals. Could fate be again at work at this late hour on this momentous evening?

3:20, 3:19, 3:18, an eternity of time for Fairaday to hold the fortress! Could they sustain it until the final gun? Coach Clements of Fairaday called a time out with 2:16 seconds on the clock. Fairaday was to kick to Simpson, and he felt it was time to settle his team down before battling out these next two minutes of eternity. He alerted them once again of the highly touted punt returner for Simpson, John Greeson. He had already committed to play at the University of Georgia next season for Vince Dooley. He was small in stature, but very speedy. "Get him early boys. Don't let him find a seam or he'll kill us!" Coach Clements had a stern look on his face for the boys to see. The boys could see a very stern look on Coach Clements' face. This was time to get serious and to hold the line!

Fairaday kicked, and sure enough, John Greeson received the ball on the Simpson 22 yard line and headed straight up field. He was bobbing and weaving his way through the defenders and was almost free when it happened. He tripped up on his own feet around the Fairaday 40 yard line and fell hard to the ground, fumbling the ball before impact. It squibbed about in several directions with five or six players for each side trying to fall on it. Finally, it was none other than little Bobby Stockton who fell on the ball and held on for dear life! Bobby had been sent into the game as a substitute at the last second. It was the first game of his career, being a ninth grader and not starting the season on varsity. He was a frail little fellow, weighing only 115 pounds, and the coach was hesitant at first whether or not to use him, but his best defender had gone down with a bad knee.

1:39, 1:38, 1:37 . . . Simpson had called all of their time-outs, all that Brad had to do was to hold onto the ball and touch his knee to the ground with each play, and Fairaday would pull the biggest upset game of the season.

Well, you may have already guessed the eventual outcome. Fairaday won that barnburner, and the town celebrated victory, holding all bragging rights for the next year. As the clock wound down the final seconds, the rains returned to an unusual extent, almost as if fate had planned it that way. It really began to pour. The Millers and others pulled out their umbrellas and ponchos as they continued to move from the stadium to their vehicles. The Millers went down to the sidelines to congratulate Brad Peterson and the other team members, along with Coach Clements. Anna Louise and Melody changed from their gowns and into their cheerleading suits after half time and had huddled together on the sidelines. Reverend Miller brought over an extra umbrella, and they all headed together to the Miller's car and home. The celebration would take place at the Millers home as soon as Brad could leave the team. There would be many things to remember from this night of all nights! A chill followed the crowd as they departed from the stadium.

Chapter Seven
Herschel Thomas Moore

Herschel Thomas Moore was barely out of bed before the door bell rang. He shuffled around in his
underwear, looking for his robe that he felt sure he had
placed on the large red recliner in the bedroom. "Where in
the dickens could it be? I know I left it on that recliner last
night! Am I startin' to lose my mind or something?"
Moore was frustrated with himself for being so lax in remembering things these days. His mind was beginning to
slip, and he worried that he wouldn't be able to take care
of himself alone much longer.

The person at the door was very persistent in ring-
ing the bell in series. When Herschel finally found his
robe on the floor of the opposite side of the bed, he hurriedly put it on and stumbled on his way to the door.
When he opened the door, there stood Barney Hodges.
Barney had worked down at the Pepsi Cola plant with
Herschel for the past thirty-two years. They had been best

buddies around Simpson and did most everything together since Herschel's wife Elizabeth had passed two years ago. Elizabeth had breast cancer of the worst variety and her death came quickly. Herschel had been completely lost without her around for he had counted on her for just about everything! Elizabeth did all of the housework and still managed to work at the Simpson High School lunch-room as a cook. She had worked at the school for twenty-eight years before having to retire with a bad back. Doctors couldn't seem to help her, so she and Herschel had to cut back on a lot of luxuries they had previously enjoyed. She was the joy of Herschel's life, the very center of his existence, and now she was gone. The hands of fate had taken her from him, and it had been extremely difficult on Herschel. These days, he had been living almost like a hermit. His house was a mess: strewn clothes everywhere, every dish in the house piled up dirty in the sink, mail stacked on the counter unopened for days . . . Herschel was a broken man, and it had been going on that way for two years now!

The kind folks at the Rocky Shoals Baptist Church in Simpson had helped Herschel for the first couple of weeks by bringing in meals and helping him spruce up the place, but since then he had let things slip. Elizabeth had been a faithful member at Rocky Shoals Baptist, but Herschel had never set foot in that church. He was raised at the Church of God but had long since lost his faith in churches completely. He was bitter with God now and blamed God for Elizabeth's passing. Somehow he just couldn't seem to find that peace that he had heard preachers talk about for years. He wondered how such a loving God could bring such devastation into a person's life! That couldn't be the God that he heard about as a child at the Church of God.

"For goodness sakes, Barney, why did you come and get me out of bed at 6:30 in the morning?" Herschel's voice was very trite and had a tinge of anger in it. "This better be good, you know!"

"Herschel, you better let me come inside and put on some coffee while you get a bath and dress. Boss just called me 'bout ten minutes ago and said that we had a new load of drinks coming at 7:30 this morning and he needed the both of us down there to open the plant before the other workers come in. I ain't lying to you, Herschel. You know how mad the old man gets when nobody's there to let those guys from the Waycross plant in! Why, he'll have our hides if we don't hurry up, Hersh!" That was Barney's endearing name for Herschel – Hersh – and he had used it since the first time they had met.

These two guys were closer than brothers. In fact, neither one had any siblings. Barney had been married once, years ago, but his wife couldn't stand his bad habits of smoking like a freight train and drinking with the boys down at Hinson's Bar every Friday and Saturday night. She had left him after only three years of marriage, and Barney had never sought another woman. He lived a moderate life on the fringes in a little shanty at the edge of Simpson and never ventured much further away from home than an occasional trip to see his Aunt Runelle in Stuckey, Georgia, or his other aunt and uncle in Romine. He was a "good ole boy" and a rock-solid worker. He had driven a delivery truck for Pepsi for the last thirteen years, covering all the little stores along the roadside in six different counties. Herschel had the only other route for deliveries, but he mostly worked the larger cities in the area. Since Herschel was the senior driver of the two, he had been given the easier route. Barney never complained for he thoroughly enjoyed his work. He always arrived early and usually left late. He could talk the horns off a bull.

At the end of each day's routes, the two would bring their trucks into the plant and have them reloaded for the following day. People out there needed their Pepsi Colas, so it was most vital that they run their routes on time. Everybody around the six county area knew old Herschel and his trusty sidekick, Barney. They were perhaps the friendliest old fellows around. They'd never hurt a flea. I guess Herschel's only vice was his cigars. He was content to drive his big old Pepsi truck each day and would prop his arm up on the driver's side door and puff away on that Swisher Sweet cigar. Why, he had at least ten boxes in that truck with him at any given time. He would never run out of cigars. People were just drawn to these two characters. They seemed to be old icons from a previous age. In fact, they actually were old, but were unwilling to admit it!

As the coffee brewed, Herschel ran around the house trying to find some clean clothes to wear. After settling on a two day old pair of jeans and a khaki shirt, he brushed quickly through the ten or twelve hairs on his head and rushed into the kitchen where Barney had two cups of coffee ready.

"Well, it's 'bout time you got ready, Hersh! If you don't hurry and drink your coffee, the old man is gonna kill us! Hurry up, for goodness sakes!" Barney was really in a hurry-up mode. Herschel just seemed to ignore him, which always made matters worse. This wasn't the first time Barney had rushed Herschel about. It was almost a daily affair. You see, Barney was Herschel's alarm clock. Old Hersh would probably never wake up in the mornings were it not for Barney.

While he sipped on his coffee, Herschel spoke up. "Barney, let me tell you somethin' 'bout life. Them damn drinks will be there whether we show up today or not! Do you think for one solitary second that old Haskins would fire us if we didn't show up on time today? You know better! We're the best two workers he's ever had! Nobody would do the work that we do without complaining a lot and constantly griping for more pay, now would they? Tell me, Barney, when was the last time that old codger gave us a raise? Three years ago? And you're rushing me to hurry up!" Herschel's voice was stern and with purpose. "Barney, you gotta get a grip on your life, son. It's passing you by quicker than you think. Sometimes I just want to throw up my hands and give it all up and then I think about what I'd do if I did. You know where I'd wind up, Barney? I'll tell you flat out. I'd be out yonder in Potter's Field at the edge of town with ten toes straight up! Since my 'Lizbeth left here, I ain't been too concerned with a lot of things, and that damn job is one of 'em, so stop your fussing and worry. Things will take care of themselves."

"Hush your mouth, Hersh. Ain't nobody gonna die today. Dog, just get it together and let's go. Drink your coffee and come on. I don't want to have to explain to old Haskins why we're late again. Besides, I want to get home today early enough to go fishin'." Barney was frustrated and always anxious and knew they would have a price to pay should they be late for work. Homer Haskins was a sullen old soul and didn't take laxness on a worker's behalf too lightly, regardless as to how long an employee had been with him. Why, it seemed that every week he would fire another worker and hire one immediately in his place. A job was never secure at the Pepsi Cola plant.

"Gosh almighty, Barney. If you're that eager to hit the road, I'll skip the dern coffee! I want you to know though that I'm gone be in a very foul mood all day because I skipped my coffee." Herschel grabbed a hand full of Swisher Sweets and stuck them in his shirt pocket as they left the house. For years, old man Haskins had given Herschel a box of 24 Swisher Sweets for his Christmas present and they had accumulated everywhere. He couldn't smoke them fast enough, what with his own purchases at Roxbury's General Store on his weekly route to Cliborn. He couldn't pass up an opportunity to buy a box from old man Chissum, especially since he was always so nice to him and gave him a deep discount on the cigars.

The two codgers jumped into Barney's old '62 Ford pickup and headed straight to the plant where they were greeted by the guys from Waycross who were there already. These were the same guys that usually came with the big tractor-trailer truck from the Waycross plant. It was necessary to supplement the bottling capacities of the Simpson plant due to its size, so a weekly run was made to avoid any shortages on the Simpson routes. Barney and old Herschel knew these guys well and always joked around with them week after week. "Hoot" Collier and "Buckshot" Williams were the two drivers, and they were quite the characters as well. They loved a good joke about as well as anyone, and Barney always had a good one for them each week.

"Hoot," Barney started, "Did you hear that Boudreau joke about Clarence?"

"Naw! You ain't never told me that one, Barney. What's it about?" Hoot asked.

Herschel lit one of his Swisher Sweets and knew this was gonna take a while. Barney had some good jokes but it took him forever to tell one. The guys started unloading, with Barney and Herschel's help, while Barney shared the joke.

"Well, you see, Boudreau, what lives down in the Louisiana Bayou, had a real mean neighbor name of Clarence what lived on the other side of the Bayou from Boudreau. They would shoot their guns across the Bayou at each other and yell nasty thangs at each other from time-to-time. Boudreau's wife, Clotile, asked Boudreau why he didn't just get in his pirogue (that's one of dem little boats they have down there) and paddle cross the bayou and whup up on Clarence and show him exactly who the man of the swamp is. Well, Boudreau turns to Clotile and says, 'Shoot fire, honey, you know what? 'Bout the time I got half way cross that bayou, one of dem big old gators would come up out of that black water and swallow me up whole! You wouldn't have no Boudreau after that. I can't do that, Clotile." The men were working feverishly to get the truck unloaded before the other workers arrived, but Barney continued with the joke.

"One day the county come and started building a bridge cross that bayou. When they finish, Clotile calls out to Boudreau and say, 'Boudreau, now you got no excuse. You git youself cross that bridge and go to Clarence and show him who the boss of the swamp is. You hear me, now go on over there.'"

"Sho nuf, Boudreau takes off cross that bridge and gets 'bout half way cross when he all of a sudden turns round and heads back to the house. Clotile asked him if he whuped up on Clarence and showed him who the man of the swamp be. Boudreau say to Clotile, 'Shoot no, woman. You know what? I git half way cross that bridge and I look up there and they got this sign that read, "Clearance – 13 Feet, 11 Inches".' Boudreau say, 'Shoot fire, honey, I never knew that man was that big!'"

At that conclusion, Hoot, Buckshot, and Herschel were laughing so hard that Herschel actually thought he was having a heart attack. That crazy Barney could tell some good ones.

Old man Haskins came in right at 8:00 AM and walked back to where the crew were unloading. "See you guys got another late start! Barney, didn't I warn you about this last week? What seems to be the problem in getting you guys here on time?" His voice was very cutting and to the point.

"Mr. Haskins, I just ain't gone lie to you. This morning when I gets up, I go out to feed my chickens and find two of them laying there with they heads off! Something got into the pen last night and had a run with them chickens. I had to fix the fence before I left or I probably wouldn't have any chickens left by tonight!" That Barney could come up with the best lies right off the top of his hat. This one was another doozy!

"I expect that you think I'm gonna believe that one, huh Barney? I thought you lost all of your chickens last year when the tornado came through and just whisked them away!" Mr. Haskins was just a bit angry in his remarks.

"No sir, you see, I did manage to keep two of my

old hens and one of the roosters. They both had a batch of biddies, not long after the tornado, and now I've got 'bout twenty chickens." With that, Haskins just let it go and told them to hurry up with the unloading so they could start their routes.

Herschel apologized to Hoot and Buckshot for being late, knowing they had a long trip back to Waycross. He then told them, "Guys, I'm so sorry, but I had the hottest little date last night and stayed out way too long with her. I think she's serious about marrying me."

Hoot, the driver of the semi, spoke up. "Herschel Moore, there ain't no woman within a thousand miles that would marry the likes of you or Barney and you know it! Who you trying to fool, old man?"

"Well, why don't you just go ask Miss Sadie Johnson 'bout that. She was my hot date for the night," Herschel replied.

Barney just had to jump into the conversation at that point. "Come on guys, let's get them damn drinks unloaded. I want to go fishin' this afternoon when I get in from my run. You guys are holdin' me up!"

Buckshot said, "Barney, you wouldn't know which end of the fishing pole to hold! Furthermore, you wouldn't know what to do with any fish you might catch."

Their conversations and shots at each other continued until the truck was fully unloaded. Hoot and Buckshot said their goodbyes and took off in their semi back to

Waycross. Herschel yelled at the two as the semi pulled away from the plant. "Hey, you two hurry back now when you don't have so long to stay! You hear?"

Herschel and Barney then went to their respective trucks and always shook hands before they left in separate directions. It was just one of their little rituals they had always done. Deep down inside, the two men knew how much they counted on each other for support and strength. What they were doing was potentially dangerous, having to face traffic all day in that heavy, oversized delivery truck. Barney knew that Herschel would have to retire in the next two years, but he kept quiet about it, not wanting to bring up the subject too soon. Besides, what would he do without old Herschel around? It would never be the same again after his retirement, and Barney knew it. He figured that that would be the saddest day of his life!

"Good morning, Herschel!" The voice spoke from the rear of the store as Herschel entered. It was Mr. Marshall, the owner of Marshall Handi-Mart on Collier Street. It was always the first stop of the day for Herschel. "Got any good stories to tell me today, Herschel?" Seems that Herschel had a way with the stories, though no one ever took them seriously. They were often filled with such bull and malarkey that people didn't take any of them to heart.

"Well, just wanted to tell you about my hot little date I had last night, Homer. Oh, she was such a beauty!" As he wheeled his delivery cart down the center aisle to the drink cases, he continued. "You know, I really hit it off with that woman. And she thinks the world of me too! Talking 'bout potential marriage, you know. What you think, Homer?"

"Herschel, you know you ain't had no date since Elizabeth left. There ain't a woman alive who would ever come close to the kind of woman Elizabeth Moore was, and that's the gospel truth! You shouldn't be makin' no remarks about another woman like that." Homer had attended church with Elizabeth for many years prior to her passing and had known her well. She was actually the best thing that ever happened in Herschel's life, and he knew it. "Why, Herschel Moore, if you cheated now on Elizabeth, she'd come back from the grave and haunt you for the rest of your sorry life!"

Herschel then said, "Homer, get a life, man. What's a man gonna do when he goes to sleep by himself every night and gets up every mornin' just to do the same old things over and over again? A man needs a woman. That's what God made them for, you know! What's wrong with an old man like me taking a liking to another woman? Elizabeth would be proud of me."

"Herschel, you know I'm just kidding with you. Can't you take a little joke? I know it gets tough out there living alone. I can't imagine what it would be like to lose Sylvia. You know, we've been married now for the past forty-eight years! Can't believe it's been that long. I want you to come to our 50th wedding anniversary, Herschel, if you will. Our kids are planning a big shindig year after next. It wouldn't be the same if you couldn't be there with us. I count you as one of my dearest and closest friends." Homer Marshall had now changed the entire tone of the previous conversation with more serious words.

Herschel replied, "Homer, old buddy, you know I feel the same way 'bout you. You know I'd be more than proud to come to that big shindig. Count me in!" With that, Herschel busied himself with placing the cans and bottles of Pepsi on the shelves in the cooler, then made his way on to the next stop. Place after place, day after day, six days a week, it had been for the past thirteen years on his route. People looked forward to his daily visits in each store, each mini-mart, each supermarket. Herschel Moore was an icon for many. You could almost set your watch by him as well. Herschel used to work in the plant on the bottling lines years ago, then he moved up to warehouse supervisor, and was eventually assigned his own delivery truck. He loved the route work and thrived on his personal relationships with the store owners and other employees. They had become his life since Elizabeth's death. The people gave him the incentive to go into work every day, and he appreciated their friendship and concern.

Herschel had grown up on a farm just outside of Simpson. His father was a sharecropper and knew all of the other farmers in the area. He learned to work alongside his father every day while they gleaned the other area farmers' fields. They would then truck the crops to the market and receive a portion of the pay. In the spring, they concentrated on plowing the many fields, putting out lime and fertilizer and land plaster, then harrowing the crops in their infancy of growth until they became ready for harvesting. Herschel was used to the simple things in life and was never allowed the privilege of going beyond the sixth grade in school. Work had to be done on the farm and there was no time for such ridiculous things as an education! He knew what his work in life was, so he set about to do it, much in the same fashion he did now. His work ethic was not something that he could be kidded about. He knew what it took for him to survive and was very critical toward those who tried to take from life what wasn't rightfully theirs. He didn't believe in welfare and always felt that those who could really use it never got it! His philosophies on life could stand up against the most able philosophers of any century. The man was simply wise beyond his education. Life, for Herschel Moore, was the only education he had ever received. He often told people that he had graduated from the "School of Hard Knocks!" and they believed him. Life had taught him everything he knew. A good day's work for a hard day's pay! You get out of life exactly what you put into it. If you're always taking from it, there won't be anything to give back. Treat others like you treat yourself and you'll be alright.

There he went, down the lonely backroads and busy highways, delivering more than just the usual cases of bottles and cans of Pepsi Cola. What Herschel Moore brought to every establishment was his homemade wisdom and philosophy. With a constant Swisher Sweet in his hand, seldom lit, Herschel would linger for the longest time at each store weaving his stories and tales about life to anyone interested in listening. That's why people loved him and admired the old man. Even the younger kids around Simpson took a liking to him. You could frequently see him handing out candy to the children at football games on Friday nights in Simpson. He always carried some Juicy Fruit chewing gum in the pockets of his faded overalls. Most children in Simpson knew that and would start running towards old Herschel when they saw him coming. He felt such pride in being able to give them SOMETHING. It was just his way of letting them know that he cared. There aren't many people left around like old Herschel Moore anymore. He's the last of a dying breed among those of our modern generation!

Chapter Eight
A Star on the Horizon

F olks around Fairaday still talk about that amazing football game between Fairaday and Simpson back in 1965. A lot has happened since then, however. Brad Peterson, Anna Louise's boyfriend, graduated last year and went off to college at Brewton Parker in Mount Vernon, Georgia, a Baptist Church institution. Brad was a member of the Fairaday Baptist Church and had only recently become a staunch believer. He had accepted the call into the ministry and was going to Brewton Parker to prepare for his future as a pastor. Anna Louise Miller gave him her blessings and complete support and promised him that she would be in daily prayer for his class work. Her father, Reverend John Henry Miller, had presented Brad with his first robe, following graduation, complete with stoles to wear on the proper occasions. Brad had become an integral part of the Miller family as well, and all were very proud of his accomplishments. He could have played football for the University of Georgia on a scholarship but chose the ministerial route instead. A man of conviction,

Reverened Miller would often say.

     Anna Louise and Melody Harper had also graduated with Brad, both graduating with honors. Anna Louise received the STAR STUDENT award, and was also the Valedictorian. Brad had helped her write her speech for graduation, and it was a huge success that blustery day in May. Graduation was held on a flatbed trailer situated on the fifty yard line on the football field. Brad would forever remember hearing Anna Louise recite some of the words to that Valedictory speech which he, for the most part, had written for her.

"Friends and fellow graduates, we are about to embark on the journey of a lifetime. The unknown lies ahead of us, but the roads are paved with preparation, with knowledge, with determination. What we have learned in the past twelve years of life will hopefully serve to guide us on our journey. There will be pit-falls and mountaintops, yet we must remain dedicated and focused on the journey. We should never allow the mundane to destroy our vision. Clearly, we move ahead and seek the goals we have set for our future. Yet, we cannot do this alone. We need the encouragement and help of our life-long friends whom we have made through the years.

"The great John Donne once said, 'No man is an island, entire of itself, for every man is part of the mainstream of life.' How very true those words are. We are part of it all, part of the very fabric of life. Our existence is part and parcel of the love our families had for one another. We are the offspring of life and must, without hesitation, move forward in the faith and confidence that our families and friends will be there for us.

"Today marks the beginning of the journey that will lead us through the remainder of our lives. Make wise choices, never fear the roadblocks, strive for perfection, and always remember who you are and where you came from. What we do with what we have learned is totally up to us.

"Our teachers have accomplished their work. They have instilled in us the desire for lifelong learning. Do not disappoint them. Continue to be studious and determined. Remember the good ole days of Fairaday High, and let those sweet and poignant memories carry you for the rest of your lives.

"Be well. Do good work. Love all, and may God bless you!"

Anna Louise received a standing ovation after completing her message. Brad's heart was overwhelmed at how well she delivered the message and was beaming from ear-to-ear. Anna Louise had chosen Mrs. Ruth Springer as her STAR TEACHER, and it was announced following her speech. Mrs. Springer had been Anna Louise's fourth grade teacher and had instilled within her that, in spite of her leukemia, her treatments and pain, she could achieve anything she wanted in life if she would continue to believe that God was beside her every step of the way. Anna Louise had long taken those words and her constant encouragement to heart. What a fitting tribute to such a sweet, sweet lady as Mrs. Springer. She had just retired last year, but Anna Louise gave her the best honor she had ever received as a teacher of forty-two years!

Anna Louise had been the picture of health now for several years, and, following graduation, she would move on to the University of Georgia where she would become part of the Redcoat Marching Band. She was a flutist, and a very good one at that.

The summer of 1965 saw a lot of changes around Fairaday. Little Bobby Stockton's car had been hit by a train passing through Fairaday, and Bobby had been crushed in it. The train carried the vehicle about 500 yards down the track before it finally came to a stop. Bobby, as you may remember, was the frail little kid who had fallen on the fumble by a Simpson punt returner, saving the game at that most crucial moment with the clock running out of time. People of Fairaday mourned Bobby's passing and filled the Fairaday United Methodist Church to over-flowing during the funeral. The entire town was in mourn-ing. Bobby had become a local hero because of the game that year and his quickness to respond to the fumble. Folks around Fairaday never forget such heroics, and they honor them more and more with each passing year. It really doesn't matter what you become later in life, folks in Fairaday will never forget those high school football games and your part in them. Little Bobby Stockton had graduated and had been working a couple of months down at Pork's Pig, a local Bar-B-Q restaurant in Fairaday.

Rachel Smith, mother of four small children, was found shot to death in her trailer on the outskirts of Fairaday. No evidence existed to link anyone to her murder, but it was assumed that her estranged husband had something to do with it. The county took the children in and placed them in foster homes. People became very suspicious of one another it seemed for awhile.

The pants factory, where Melody's mother had worked for so many years, folded up and left town like a carnival, leaving over 200 employees without work. Mrs. Harper was lucky to get a job at the plant in Simpson, however, actually making more money than before. Melody was now attending college at Valdosta State, majoring in Early Childhood Education. She had always dreamed of growing up to be just like Mrs. Miller. Her grades were good enough to secure various scholarships to the college and to live on campus without it taking such a strain on her mother's finances. She was an exemplary student, from start-to-finish, and her mother was so very proud of what she had been able to accomplish in such little time.

Jason, the Miller's son, was now playing football and baseball at the Fairaday high school, excelling in both sports. He was catcher on the baseball team with a very high average of .425. He was the team's Homerun King. He played defensive end on the football team and actually stood a strong chance of getting a full-scholarship the following year, however, his heart and soul was in baseball and would accept whatever offers came in that sport.

Although a great distance separated Melody, Anna Louise, and Brad, they seemed to coordinate their returns to Fairaday without any problems. Weekends would be filled with dates, movies, and church. Usually, they would double-date; Melody and Heath Trulock, Anna Louise and Brad. Heath was also a 1965 graduate with Melody, Brad and Anna Louise. He was a tight end on the football team with Brad, and the two were very close friends. Heath had been fond of Melody for years and had finally asked her out on the night of graduation. Melody had accepted without reservations. Mrs. Harper approved of Heath, who was now working at the local Piggly Wiggly store in the meat department. He never had desires for college, so he did what most young men in Fairaday do when they do not go to college—he worked. He was a very nice and polite young man and had won the hearts of women who shopped the meat market at the "Pig."

Brad had been given a call by a small country Baptist Church near Mount Vernon while in his first semester at Brewton Parker. They wanted to know if he would be interested in serving as their interim pastor until a full-time pastor could be called. In actuality, they liked his preaching so much that they were not in any hurry to call anyone else! It was a great match for Brad, and he excelled in the pulpit and in his studies at college. He had quite a way with the youth of the church and the group had grown dramatically in the first few months of his pastorate there.

Brad's ministry really changed things around Fairaday. He would rarely be coming home now on the weekends unless the church gave him a Sunday off. It wasn't long before Melody, Heath, and Anna Louise began making their way to Mount Vernon to hear Brad preach and to spend time with him there. A boarding house in town supplied a place for the three to room, and the situation worked out well for awhile. Anna Louise became a bit limited from her visits to Mount Vernon because of her band position at the University. She had to travel to all the away games to other states and to be present to play in the band every Saturday during football season in Athens. That placed a great strain on her relationship with Brad, but he understood completely. This went on for the next three years.

Brad was eventually ordained deacon by the little church and received his License to Preach the Gospel. He had bought a frame, and had put his license in it, and had hung it up on his dorm wall. He was so proud of that accomplishment and so was Anna Louise and the Millers. Pastor John couldn't say enough good things about Brad, and secretly hoped that he would be Anna Louise's choice for marriage one day. Margie Miller had agreed.

Chapter Nine
Barney's Missing

Herschel finished his route and slumbered home for another lonely night in front of the TV and thought about perhaps asking his neighbor, Bennie Hessman, to come over and play a round of cards. Bennie was good about coming over from time to time to help keep Herschel occupied. Bennie liked to cheat a lot, so Herschel wasn't even sure if he'd invite him over on this particular night. Bennie always found their card games an escape from his wife's constant bickering. Since he had broken his leg at work two months ago, she had been a constant pain in his craw. She wanted him back to work A.S.A.P. He was driving her crazy, she said, and must go back to work soon or she was going to lose it. The doctors had told him that it would be a couple of more weeks before Bennie could go back, and she was buying her time in anticipation.

Bennie was alright, but, as the official and only token Jew in town, he had some really weird quirks about him. Herschel felt a little uncomfortable around him, especially when Bennie would start talking about religion. Herschel was never a very religious man, although he did believe in a supreme being. Elizabeth had always been the faithful one to attend church, but not Herschel. He would only attend with her on occasion—you know—like Christmas Sunday, Easter Sunday or Homecoming. He usually had problems with the local pastors that served in the churches around Simpson. He felt that they should get out and find a job like other normal people. It would be alright for them to preach on Sunday, but they still needed to "work", he thought.

Soon as Herschel came through his front door, here came Bennie from across the road, hobbling along on his crutches at two-tenths of a mile per hour. He yelled out to Herschel: "Hey, Herschel! Want to play cards tonight? I've got a new game to teach you. You're gonna really like it, too. What about it? Want to play?"

Herschel knew that Bennie was just trying to get out of the house again, but he let Bennie come on over. He had stopped by the local Kentucky Fried Chicken place and had gotten himself a two piece all white chicken dinner with a jalapeno pepper! That was his favorite meal of all meals. He placed the chicken box on the kitchen table while he awaited Bennie's slow entrance.

"What you got there, Herschel?" Bennie asked.

"Oh, just a box of chicken for supper," Herschel responded.

"Gonna ask me to join you?" Bennie inquired.

"Now, Bennie, you know that you've already had

your supper. Your wife feeds you at five o'clock every day. Why do you want to beg from a poor man for his supper? You ought to be ashamed of yourself!" Herschel meant it with heart.

Bennie laughed at Herschel's remarks. "I love to get you all riled-up, Herschel. I can see the smoke coming out of your nostrils when you do. Yes, I've already eaten supper. Margaret served me some rutabagas, purple hull butterbeans, fresh made biscuits, and cube steak for dinner." He was rubbing all of that in for Herschel's benefit, since his little chicken box was so meager. Herschel had always sworn to the knowledge that Jewish people were always spouting off about their riches and their abilities to do better than most folk. It irritated the dickens out of Herschel. "Go ahead and enjoy your little meal while I turn on your TV and get our card table set up. Hope that Jalapeno pepper gets you hot tonight cause you're gonna need it in order to beat me!"

In the middle of eating his chicken breast, after having finished off the wing, the telephone rang. It was about 7:30 PM at that point as Herschel glanced down at his watch, wondering who could be calling him at this hour.

"Herschel," the voice on the other end answered to his hello. "It's Johnny Rogers with the Civil Defense. I need to know if you've seen Barney this afternoon."

"No," Herschel replied. "I haven't seen him since we left the plant this morning in separate directions. What's going on?"

"Well, we got a call a little while ago from a couple who said that Barney had been down at Statham's Landing this evening and had been fishing. Somebody fittin' his description had jumped into the whirl-hole in the bend of the creek to save a mother and a little girl from drowning. The man hadn't been seen since. I thought that since Barney don't have a telephone in that shack of his, that maybe you could go over there and see if he was home." Herschel's heart suddenly dropped! He then remembered that Barney had told him that morning that he hoped to get off in time today to go fishing. The Waycross delivery boys had made light of his fishing abilities, but Barney was a dang good fisherman and took his fishing very seriously.

"Johnny, he did say that he was planning to go fishing this afternoon after he got off work, but he didn't say where in particular." Herschel's voice trembled as he spoke. A million thoughts began to rush through his brain about his best friend. He told Bennie to go back home because he had to leave to check on Barney.

"Herschel, can you come down to Statham's Landing and help us out?" Herschel could tell by Johnny's tone of voice that he was desperate at this point. "We only got a couple of guys down here, and everybody else is tied-up with other things in town. Please, if you can, come down and help us if you will. Go by Barney's house on your way and check to make sure whether he's home or not. Remember to bring your flashlight. It's as dark as hell down here!"

"I'm on my way," Herschel answered. With that, he quickly jumped up from the table and put his shoes back on, telling Bennie goodbye and also what had happened as reported by Johnny. "Bennie, close the door behind you. I've got to go help them find whoever's drowned in the creek. I hope and pray it's not Barney. If it is, they think he's still in the creek."

Herschel went by Barney's house and found no lights on and no response at the front door. He then jumped back into his pickup and hurried down Highway 56 to where Statham's Landing crossed. He turned down a little pulpwood road that swimmers and fishermen used to get to the creek. It was a good ways up the road, and it had been raining hard that evening, so the road was slick and muddy. At the end of the road was Statham's Landing where the creek formed a large pool of water and swirled down the creek at this point, creating a whirl hole. The creek was good for catching world class redbreast, and it wouldn't surprise Herschel at all if that crazy Barney had come down here to fish. "God," he said under his breath, "Don't let it be my buddy! Please, God, don't let it be Barney!"

As Herschel approached the open area at the end of the road, he could see several cars parked in different directions along the banks of the creek. He also saw the big lights of the Civil Defense crew set up on the banks and shining down into the murky dark waters of the whirl hole area. People were clamoring everywhere, all hoping to see some action. The Civil Defense workers, two of them, were throwing in a drag line with hooks on the end hoping to retrieve a body. Each return gave them little hope that the body was still in this area. Perhaps it had drifted on further down the creek, they were beginning to believe. Perhaps old Barney will come walking out of the swamp after awhile with a string full of bluegill and redbreast, Herschel thought to himself. He had looked over among the cars and trucks and had sighted Barney's old truck. His heart took a heavy jolt when he saw the truck they went to work in every morning and came home in each evening. Yep, Barney's here somewhere, he thought.

Herschel turned to Johnny Rogers and told him that Barney's truck was over near the sweet gum trees at the edge of the road. He had to be around here somewhere. Johnny affirmed that he had already investigated the truck and knew that it was Barney's before he had called Herschel. That's why the concern.

Johnny then said to one of the workers, "I'm sorry, guys, but it's been four hours now, and we've not found anyone yet. They said that whoever it was had managed to save a little girl and her mother from drowning out there in the middle of the whirl hole, but then he couldn't save himself."

Herschel thought of how much that sounded like Barney, an unselfish person who was always thinking of others.

"Sounds just like something that Barney would do. Right, Herschel?" Johnny asked.

"Yea, I'm afraid it does. Barney never knows

when to say no. I pray to God that's not him down there."
Herschel's voice was quivering as he spoke with tears
streaming down his face. "He's my best buddy, and I can't
live without him, guys! We've got to find him alive!"

With one last toss of the grappling hooks, one of
the workers shouted out. "Wait! I think I've got something." Apparently his hooks had connected with something heavy under the water. He was very near the edge
when he engaged the hooks into something big.

Harold Jones put on his scuba gear at that point
and dropped down into the swirl just off the bank. Knowing now where the object was, he followed the grappling
line to the bottom of Statham's Creek. The hole was approximately 30 feet deep at that point where the waters
had churned through many generations. It wasn't long before Harold returned to the surface with a body. It was old
Barney! His skin was whiter than light with a bluish tint.
The two Civil Defense workers strained to get his body
onto the bank with Herschel's help. Herschel then lost it
completely, fell to Barney's side, and started crying like a
baby.

"Barney, you crazy old fool, why did you do it?
Why? Why did you go into the water knowing full well
you couldn't swim?" Herschel was beside himself, and the
workers were trying to console him.

"Do you mean to tell us that Barney couldn't
swim, Herschel?" Johnny Rogers asked.

"That's right. He was always afraid of the water
for as long as I've known him. Loved to fish, but was

afraid of the water. He knew he couldn't swim, dammit! Why did he jump in there to save those two if he knew he couldn't swim?" Herschel was nearly hysterical at this point, so the two workers asked him to go sit in their truck while they got Barney onto a stretcher. "You gonna take him to Memorial Funeral Home, guys?" Herschel asked.

"Yea, Herschel. We'll take good care of him. Do you know his family?"

"Don't got any," Herschel said as he walked towards the truck. "Just me, I guess."

The Civil Defense truck pulled away with Barney's body as Herschel stood by and watched the last glimmer of light leaving the swamp. It was like the very light of his soul had departed and left him. How would he possibly carry on now without Barney, his best buddy? He was the only person that made his life and work at the Pepsi plant bearable since Elizabeth's death two years ago. Now he's gone! Barney's gone so quickly. He won't be there in the morning when we shake hands and pull out to run our routes, he thought.

Herschel caught up with the Civil Defense truck and followed it into town to Memorial Funeral Home. The funeral home had already been contacted by radio that Barney's body was being brought in, so Mr. Albert Hopkins, director of Memorial and our local cornoner, met Herschel at his truck before he could get parked good.

"Herschel, I know you're hurting and you're probably wondering if there's anything you can do right now for Barney. Well, the best thing for you to do is to go on home and try to call as many of his friends as you can to let them know what has happened. I'll need you to come down first thing in the morning to help make plans for his funeral service. You understand, Herschel?" Mr. Hopkins had always been a good friend of Herschel's through the years and had handled Elizabeth's funeral with great respect and care. Herschel knew that Barney was in the best of care at this point, and so nodded his head in an approving fashion without saying a word. He was still in total shock. He felt completely numb from his head to his toes. He cranked his old truck and headed back home to find several of his neighbors on his front porch. They had already heard the news and came to console Herschel, knowing that Barney was his best friend. Miss Clements, at the end of the street, had brought some tea and a freshly baked cake. Mary Carter and her husband Zack brought some chicken and dumplings. Others filed in and out of Herschel's place for the next several hours bringing things and just dropping in to say how sorry they were for Barney's death. It consoled him a bit, but nothing could take away the pure pain he felt at that moment in his life. He couldn't talk to people. He really didn't know anything to say to them. Barney was gone. Final.

That night, Herschel called old man Haskins at home to tell him the news about Barney and that neither of them would be in to work the next day. Mr. Haskins would just have to let two of the young new boys take their routes for them.

"Herschel, you alright?" Mr. Haskins asked. "You

gonna be alright, Herschel? I'm so sorry about Barney. I know that I've kidded you guys for many years, but I depend upon you in the greatest ways to be the heart and soul of our plant. Everybody knows and loves the both of you, and Barney is gonna be sorely missed, I grant you that. Tell me what we can do to help."

"Mr. Haskins, guess there ain't nothing anybody can do for Barney right now. He's gone. We just gonna have to make do the best we can for the time being. We gotta get Barney buried now, so I'll see you when I can." With that, Herschel bid Mr. Haskins a good night because somebody else was at the front door knocking.

The next two days were sad days around Simpson. People mourned the loss of ole Barney, and talk spread about his death over a six county area. On the night of the visitation, you could hardly get inside the funeral home for the droves of people who came from everywhere. Shop keepers, store owners, people from every walk of life came to pay their respects to old Barney. As Herschel stood by the casket, people would speak to him about how much they liked old Barney and how he had brought much joy into their lives these past many years. Although their sympathies were appreciated, Herschel didn't really hear them. He was still thinking about Barney jumping into that swirling stream to save a little girl and her mother from drowning. "Crazy, crazy ole Barney," he kept thinking. "He couldn't swim. The fool knew he couldn't swim!"

On the day of the funeral, one was lucky to find a

seat in the chapel which would hold approximately 300 people. Folks came from six counties and beyond to pay tribute to old Barney, and it deeply warmed Herschel's heart. Believe it or not, Mr. Haskins even shut down the plant on the day of the funeral, and all the workers were there in force for the ceremony. He had contacted Mr. Hopkins at the funeral home and assured him that the workers would all serve as pallbearers or honorary pall-bearers. The preacher from Elizabeth's church, Dr. Harold Brinson, was contacted and agreed to do the funeral service. Herschel thought he had done an exceptional job, but the pastor really didn't know his buddy Barney and was limited as to what he could say directly about Barney.

The outpouring of love for this old fellow was something to witness. If Barney had only known, while he was still living, that people cared this much about him, he would have probably changed some of his ways, been more involved in things, and lived life a bit differently. But then again, that wouldn't have been the Barney every-one knew and loved.

As Herschel was leaving Barney's grave in the cemetery, he noticed a lady and her little girl over by one of the large oak trees that lined the road through the center of the cemetery. The lady waved for Herschel to come over to where they were standing in the shade. As he approached her, he noticed that she was poorly attired and so was the little girl. They had apparently not been at the funeral service but had made it to the graveside ceremony and stood off in the distance. She introduced herself to

Herschel.

"Mr. Moore, you don't know me, I'm sure, but I'm Clara Black and this here little one is Jody, my only child. We live over on the Hill place in one of Mr. Hills' little houses. I do all the housework for the Hills' and they pay me a little each week to live off of." Her voice was trembling mightily as she spoke. "I just wanted you to know that it was Mr. Barney who saved our lives the other night at the creek. We wanted to thank somebody for that miracle, and we guessed you was the best one to tell it to."

Herschel's heart was pounding rapidly as he asked, "You're the ones he saved from drowning?"

"Yes sir, we are, and we just wanted you to know how thankful we are for what Mr. Barney did for us. Nobody's ever done anything that brave for us before. My husband left us four years ago and moved off to South Carolina, and we've been strugglin' mightily to make ends meet. We was fishing that evening at the creek to catch our supper. Little Missy fell into the swirl so I jumped in to save her. I got all choked up with water trying to bring her back to the shore, but I couldn't make it and started drowning. Fore I knew it, these hands were all over me and Missy, and they was pulling us on to the shore. I thought at first that it was the hands of God helping us poor folks out of the water, but then I turned and finally saw his face. It was rough shaven with wrinkles and lines and a great big smile. Bout that time, he slipped and fell back into the swirl, and it took him right down. We looked and looked and looked, but he never did pop back up! We was the only other people down at the creek at the time, and my little Missy went running down the dirt road back up to the highway to see if she could get somebody down there to help us. This man come along and brought Missy with him back to the creek where I was waiting. Mister Herschel, I was scared to death that Mister Barney had drowned and that it cost him his life to save the two of us."

Both Clara and Missy then reached out to hug Herschel, and he gladly took them into his arms. They were both in tears and Herschel could hardly stand it. His heart was breaking for them and for Barney. His emotions were so mixed up at that point that he knew no other way to respond than to stand there and envelope them in his arms.

Little Missy spoke up at that point. "Mister Barney saved my life. I'm gonna live the rest of my life for him." Oh, what pain those words brought to Herschel's heart.

Herschel asked if he could give the two a ride back out to the Hill place, and they gladly accepted. They had walked to town and to the cemetery, about a four mile journey, and he wasn't about to leave the last remaining fragments of Barney's life in that condition. He drove them by Kentucky Fried Chicken and bought a big box of chicken and fixings for their supper and asked if he could share supper with them at their home once they returned. Clara Black had agreed, and so off they went.

In the weeks to come, Herschel paid several more visits to the Hill place to check on this special couple. It wasn't long before he invited them to come and live with him in Simpson. He would pay Clara to help him keep his house straight and to cook the meals while he went to work. Little Missy wasn't in school yet, and so it would work out great if she would accept the offer. Herschel wasn't concerned with what folks might say or think in town. He was only concerned with their well being.

Clara Black accepted the offer, and severed her relationship with the Hills'. She and Missy then moved in with Herschel. It was only a platonic relationship for them, and Herschel never once considered anything more. He was too much of a gentleman. He spent money buying them new clothes, and Clara had him buying materials so she could spruce up the old house and make it look new. He got her a hair appointment down at Martha's Cuts and Curls and he swore when he picked her up that she was totally transformed into a beautiful young lady now. Indeed, her appearance had changed from somber to radiant!

A month later, Herschel asked Clara to marry him, and she accepted without reservation. Who would have ever thought that this old timer would ever find a woman again who would accept him and love him as he was? Why, Clara and Missy even got old Herschel back to church. They went together every Sunday out to the little Blue Springs Baptist Church near the Hill place where Clara and Missy had been going for a few months. They were welcomed with open arms in that little church, and Herschel began to feel at home back where he belonged.

Herschel took two weeks of his accumulated vacation time (since he never used it through the years) and took both Clara and Missy on a honeymoon/vacation down to Panama City Beach, Florida. The three had the time of their lives! Herschel often thought about how all of this had transpired, and the fact that had it not been for Barney's unselfish quest that evening, he would have never found salvation and the joy that Clara and Missy had brought into his life.

Barney had made a choice that fateful afternoon. In a split-second, between here and eternity, all of life hung in the balance. One man, one decision. Barney chose the only route given to him. Sacrificing his own life, he jumped into the swirling black and murky waters of Statham's Creek and saved those two people, never thinking once about himself and the fact that he couldn't swim! Fate came knocking, and Barney answered the door. There were three souls saved that evening at the creek.

Chapter Ten
Graduation Time, Again!

In May of 1971, the Millers loaded up their Suburban for another momentous occasion. They were on their way to Athens for Anna Louise's graduation from the University of Georgia. She had majored in speech therapy and had also lettered in band all four years. The Millers couldn't have been more proud of her accomplishments. She had wanted to work with small school children with speech impediments, and help them to overcome their disabilities. The Millers were to stop in Mount Vernon and pick up Brad Peterson on their way to Athens for the Saturday graduation. He would have to be back that night in order to preach at his church on Sunday morning. Melody would be graduating from Valdosta State that same morning, so she would not be making the trip with the Millers. The Millers had relayed their congratulations to Amanda Harper before leaving town and told Amanda to give Melody a great big hug for them at her graduation. They left a graduation gift for Melody with Mrs. Harper.

As they headed out for Mount Vernon the day before graduation, Jason spoke up and said, "I can't believe it! My little sister is graduating from college, three years ahead of me! Some things just don't seem fair," he muttered. Jason was playing on a baseball scholarship at Valdosta State where Melody attended school. He and Melody saw each other often, and they had kept one another company on many occasions.

"Well, you better believe it, Jason," Pastor John Henry Miller stated. "Your sister doesn't let the grass grow under her feet. She came into this life in a whirlwind and she'll make the most of it while she's here. That's quite a girl we have, and quite a sister to you as well. And, what's with this 'little sister' stuff? She's your BIG sister, Jason."

The ride to Athens, through Mount Vernon, was long and arduous. It did allow the Millers and Brad time to talk somewhat about the future and any plans that he and Anna Louise may have discussed. Brad mentioned going to Seminary the following year and how it would take three years to complete, eventually receiving his Master of Divinity degree at the end. He planned to attend Wake Forest in North Carolina, which meant that he would be further away from Fairaday than he had been from Mount Vernon. Pastor Miller thought that was an excellent seminary of choice and commended him for choosing it.

"Of course, we haven't discussed it with you guys," Brad interjected, "But we have actually talked about the possibility of getting married in the fall, just before I have to leave for Wake Forest and my first semester. It should be perfect timing for the both of us. Anna Louise could find a position in her field somewhere in the area around Wake Forest, and I will secure a pastorate in a local church that may be looking for a pastor. Then I can begin concentrating on my studies and preaching each weekend, and Anna Louise can follow her dream at the same time. The seminary will actually help Anna Louise secure a job in order for her to support me as a student. What do you guys think about that?"

Mrs. Miller was the first to speak. "Do you mean to tell me, Mr. Brad Peterson, that you are asking for our daughter's hand in marriage? If you are, then you are going about it in a very conniving way, don't you think?"

Pastor John joined in. "That's O.K., Brad. Margie doesn't quite understand how these things work for us guys. If what you are truly asking for is Anna Louise's hand in marriage, then you certainly know that you have our blessings. We think the world of you, and your career is firmly in hand. You'll make an excellent husband to our daughter."

"Are you aware of all that has happened in Anna Louise's life, Brad?" Mrs. Miller was getting very serious at this point, the caring mother syndrome at work. "Do you realize that the hand of God has been on our little girl since her birth and has brought her through so many difficulties and changes in her life? Has she told you about the

leukemia that's now in remission, her premature birth, her
long road each time to recovery?"

Boy, the air was really getting thin in that Suburban at that moment! Mrs. Miller was really picking for
Brad's most heartfelt responses before she would relent
and give her permission to Brad for marriage.

"Yes, Mrs. Miller, she has told me everything. In
fact, we talk about those miracles every time we're together and how God has brought us together and has kept
us together since early high school. I love her, Mrs.
Miller, and want to be there for her the rest of her life.
You can count on me to provide for her and to help sustain her through the years to come. I will never let you
guys down in that department, rest assured!" Brad was
almost in tears when he finished.

"Brad, you're my kind of son-in-law, and I gladly
welcome you, dear, into our family," Margie responded
with a smile upon her face. "You've already been a major
part of our family now over the past few years, and we
would be lost without you."

Brad felt a great burden lift from his shoulders
with Margie's response. Mrs. Miller seemed no longer
hesitant, but one could tell her great concern over Anna
Louise's health.

"Anna Louise may seem fine to you at the present,
but God only knows when the next attack will happen. It's
been nearly twelve years now since she entered remission,
but it could happen any time. We're trusting that it never
will, but none of us can be assured that it won't. I believe

that Anna Louise is very strong at the present, but no one knows what the future brings.

"I guess my greatest concern would be for you, Brad," Mrs. Miller continued. "Would it be fair to you if in two years, ten years, or whenever, Anna Louise's cancer returned and put a burden and hardship on you?"

"Mrs. Miller," Brad responded, "I love Anna Louise with all of my heart, and we have prayed together through every possible scenario. We are now willing to share our lives together forever, even if that forever is a few days, months or years. We'll take whatever time we have together and make the most of it."

Reverend Miller pulled the Suburban off to the side of the road. He and Margie turned towards the back seat, joining hands with Brad and Jason, while Reverend Miller led them in a prayer.

"Lord, we know that it is your will for Brad to be in Anna Louise's life, and we accept that. We pray that right now you will bind them together with your tender grace and mercy and grant them your wonderful peace from this moment forward. Amen." At that, everyone in the vehicle said "Amen."

The road to Athens, Georgia, became a lot shorter now that Brad had gotten that heavy weight off his shoulders. Small discussions of potential wedding plans ensued. Which church? Which pastor? You know, the usual wedding details that had to be attended to. If they were planning a wedding for the fall, and this was May, some things had to be resolved almost immediately. There was no time to lose, especially from Mrs. Miller's viewpoint. Invitations. Dresses for the bride and bridesmaids, the attendants, etc. Wedding cake. The reception dinner. The wedding reception. What a headache, she thought, as she mused hour on end, but what a blessing to have such a wonderful young man with a great future as her son-in-law! He understood Anna Louise's special needs and her physical condition and accepted her completely the way she was. She was the proverbial apple-of-his-eye! How could she be more happy for them?

When they arrived at the motel in Athens, they called Anna Louise, and she bounded down there to meet them immediately. She was so excited to see everyone.

"Hey, guys, you all made it! You look so good and wonderful. I'm the luckiest girl on the face of this earth!" Turning to Brad, she gave him a great big hug and said, "How's my soon-to-be-seminarian?"

"Great, honey! Guess what?" he asked her.

"What is it Brad?" Anna Louise conjectured.

"Your folks and I have the wedding almost planned out to a tee! We've talked about it all the way up here, and they've both granted me your hand in marriage. Will you marry me, Anna Louise Miller?" With that question, Brad fell to his knees, in that motel room, with his hands clasped together in front of her.

"Get up, silly. Of course I'll marry you! I'm so happy that I could die right now and be the most blessed person on earth! I thought you'd never ask! Now, we've got to get through this graduation thing together and then attend yours next week at Brewton Parker. Are you ready for your finals week?"

"I think I'll manage," Brad responded with a sheepish grin. In fact, he was to graduate at the head of his class—Valedictorian! The Millers were so proud of this young man who seemed perfect in every possible way. God had really blessed them with such a fine future son-in-law.

No doubt about it, they were both in heaven already! Brad's parents would be next in line to learn of the good news as soon as they returned home to Fairaday.

"Could we wait guys until next weekend at my graduation to break the news to my folks? In fact, could we just plan an evening meal together at this great little restaurant in Vidalia, just a few miles from Mount Vernon? There we could share the news around the dinner table." Brad was really serious about not breaking the news to anyone until then. The Millers all agreed.

"Thanks guys. You are all so very special to me. You've helped me through a lot over these past years, and I will be eternally grateful to you, not only for giving me such a beautiful bride-to-be, but for your friendship, support, and concern." Brad couldn't have been happier than at that moment. Everything in his life was finally coming together. He had been distraught over not accepting the football scholarship to quarterback at the University of Georgia; he would always wonder where that could have possibly landed him up the road. Yet, he had felt the call into ministry far greater than playing football for a living. Choices. Always tough choices to make in life! Life is full of them, around every bend in the road. God had a plan for his life, and, at this moment, it included this beautiful young Georgia graduate, whom he embraced and hugged tightly.

"Don't squeeze so hard, Brad!" Anna Louise said. "Don't forget that I'm not a tackle on the defense. I will break, you know!"

"I'm sorry, Hon. I am just so happy that I cannot contain myself." Brad was certainly on cloud-nine. They all went over to the Commons that evening to make the final preparations for Anna Louise's graduation the following morning. She had one last practice with the Redcoat Marching Band that night, for they would perform at the graduation ceremony. This would be Anna Louise's last responsibility to the band which had helped her through her college career. It was the very least she could do in service.

The following morning, Saturday, The Millers and Brad sat proudly in the stands as they watched Anna Louise and the band enter the field and play an opening rendition of "Glory, Glory, Hallelujah!" Following that, a minister offered a prayer, and then the President of the University gave a brief five minute speech on character and what a wonderful class this was to be honoring the University of Georgia by completing their requirements. The band then played the National Anthem while everyone saluted the flag in the end zone. Quite ironic for Brad, who could have easily played football here and been close to Anna Louise the last four years, but fate led him in another direction. He watched the processional of graduates walk then to their respective seats, which were arranged in rows on the field. He was so proud of her, as were the Millers.

The graduation went as expected. When all had been packed and ready, the Suburban pulled out of Athens, Georgia, headed back by Mount Vernon to drop Brad off at Brewton Parker. They would all return the following Saturday for Brad's graduation and would afford him the same support that they had given Anna Louise.

After they had deposited Brad, plans quickly began developing for the upcoming marriage. Not much time, Mrs. Miller thought. They would have to work hurriedly to get things into place. Anna Louise mentioned that Brad's birthday would be on Saturday, September 10, and what a wonderful time to plan a wedding for!

"Now you just wait a darn minute, Anna Louise Miller. We are already pushed to the limit with getting this thing under control and planned. How can you possibly set it that soon?" Mrs. Miller was a wee bit perturbed with Anna Louise at this point, and it showed in her tone of voice.

"Mom, please calm down. It'll work out just fine, you'll see. God has everything in control, just like you've always taught me for the past twenty-one years of my life. He'll work this out as well." Anna was almost in tears.

"I'm sorry, dear, but all of this news just came as a shock to me yesterday and today. I couldn't even concentrate on enjoying your graduation this morning without thinking about the myriad of things yet to be done. I want it to be just perfect for my little girl. You know how I am, and this will be my only daughter's wedding and my only chance to get it right! You'll just have to overlook a lot of what I say." Mrs. Miller was a bit saddened in her tone of voice at this point.

Jason, who had been sitting quietly in the backseat reading, spoke up with his usual sarcastic animation. "Mean to tell me that you're serious about marrying that bum, Brad Peterson? He'll be my brother-in-law? My word, Sis, I don't know if I can handle that or not! Seems mighty scary to me!"

"Jason, I love you dearly, Brother, but there comes a time in every girl's life when she has to break her brother's heart. This is one of them for me. I do appreciate your concern, but you well know that Brad Peterson is not a BUM! You are rotten, brother of mine!" Anna said quite fondly with jest.

"O.K., O.K., do I get to take part in the wedding? I mean, like do I usher, light the candles, walk down the aisle and all that stuff?" Jason asked.

"You better believe it, little brother. You'll be right there in my wedding as one of the most important people in my life," Anna responded. Jason smiled at her.

Conversations about the wedding waned within a

few miles. Jason fell asleep with his head on Anna's shoulder, just like they used to do when traveling with the family as children. The Millers looked into the back seat and saw their two precious children, now practically grown and on their own, and smiled that accepting smile at each other. They had done well in raising Anna Louise and Jason. They took great pride in the outcome and felt that God had blessed the both of them, and they had not forgotten it. Life had been good.

The family pulled into the driveway at the Methodist parsonage around midnight on Saturday, tired and worn to a frazzle. Reverend Miller stayed up a while longer than the rest polishing his sermon for the coming morning. He had two messages on the answering machine about a lady in the church who had been hospitalized, and he would attend to her first thing in the morning. For now, he needed rest. He had been driving, it seemed, for two straight days and was road weary. When he finally laid his head on his pillow, he listened to Margie's breathing, and uttered a small prayer to God of thankfulness for bringing his family home again together. As he then turned and looked upon Margie's face, with the dim street light bouncing in on her form, he remembered all of the ups and downs they had shared through the years, and the abundant blessings of God upon their lives. She had been more than his soul mate, she had been his life!

Chapter Eleven
Melody's Engagement

Anna Louise could hardly wait to get home and rush over to talk with Melody about everything, including graduation, but more particularly, the upcoming wedding. Melody answered the door and immediately they embraced each other right there on the porch. They danced up and down and congratulated each other for graduating.

"Well . . . so tell me," Melody asked, "Are you finally a full-fledged speech therapist, young lady?"

"Yes, I truly am, Melody," answered Anna Louise. "Everything is now official. How did *your* graduation go yesterday?"

"Went great! I finished with honors, but missed being the Salutatorian by three-tenths of a point! Can you believe that, three-tenths of a lousy point! But I was so happy that it was finally over. Now maybe Heath and I can get serious about our wedding plans." Excitement abounded in Melody's voice, but she would also resound momentarily in Anna Louise's.

Anna Louise responded, "Are you serious, girl-friend? I didn't know that you guys were even thinking about that yet."

"As serious as a heart attack!" Melody said. Heath and I are looking at some time in the early fall. He has moved up as the meat market manager now at Piggly Wiggly, and his salary is much better than before. I've made application for a teacher's position at Tompkin's Elementary, and should hear something during the summer. There are two vacancies over there, as your mom could probably tell you, and I'm hoping that she will put in a good word for me." Melody's excitement showed in her voice, as she still swirled around and around on the porch with Anna Louise.

"Hey, girlfriend, listen to this. Brad and I announced OUR wedding plans to my parents for the fall as well while we were in Athens for my graduation. Brad asked my parents for my hand in marriage while they were on their way to Athens on Friday. They, of course, approved, and we talked about our plans while at graduation and all the way home to Fairaday. We are planning a September 10th wedding, which is also Brad's birthday. Can you believe it? We're getting married in just three months time!! Mom, of course, is having a hissy over the whole thing, and making it more complicated than it needs to be."

Anna Louise stopped spinning around on the porch

for a moment and developed a very serious look on her face as she spoke to Melody. "Melody, dear, would you possibly consider the both of us having a double-ceremony? I just thought of the idea, and you can say no if you would rather not, and it won't break my heart, but wouldn't that just be awesome?"

"Sounds wonderful to me, Anna Louise, but I'll have to pass it by Heath and my mother first before we make any final decisions. That would really be cool, wouldn't it?" Melody had become excited about the prospects, but was hesitant to say yes at the moment. She was a very level headed young lady, and would have to cover all the bases before making a final decision on the matter. She began to imagine sharing the most special day of her life with her life long friend, Anna Louise Miller. After all, the two of them had been closer than two peas in a pod since birth. It would certainly make the preparations a lot easier as well. Not to mention that Anna Louise was also thinking about Mrs. Harper having to delve out a lot of her hard-earned cash for a fancy wedding for Melody. This way, they could split the costs, and the excitement. What a novel idea! The wheels were really spinning in each of their heads.

The two girls were now jubilant at the possibilities. Childhood friends would be sharing the most important day of their lives together.

The following weekend found the Millers in

Mount Vernon for Brad's graduation. It was a joyous occasion, especially now that Brad figured into the family's future as son-in-law. Of course, the Petersons were there, and it was during the evening meal, following graduation, that Brad and Anna Louise made their announcement to all who had gathered. They had settled on the 10th of September as the date. Brad would then begin classes at Wake Forest on the 21st of September, allowing them enough time to move into a house and to get situated. Brad told them that he had already secured a lease on an apartment near the campus, and the school was checking into possible job opportunities for Anna Louise in the local area. Everything was set, except for the wedding plans.

It was at that time that Anna Louise announced the plans for a double-wedding with Melody and Heath. She and Brad had discussed the matter with Melody, Heath, and Mrs. Harper, and they had gladly accepted the idea. Mrs. Miller, of course, showed again her concern!

"How in the world could you guys possibly think that we can get everything ready in time for ONE wedding, let alone a DOUBLE wedding?" Mrs. Miller was beside herself, and her voice sounded helpless.

"Mom, don't worry. Mrs. Harper will be working hand-in-hand with you. She has also agreed to do all of the party favors and the cooking for the reception. You know how good she is at that, so we'll be fine! Just calm down and get into the flow of things." Anna Louise always looked at the lighter side of everything. Nothing was impossible with that girl. She was scatter-brained at times, but always centered on what was right.

"O.K. dear, you just know that I always like everything to be perfect. Give me a little space and I'll get myself together. Amanda and I will work out the major details, and your father has agreed to do the ceremony." Margie Miller had finally calmed down at this point, and she seemed to be more accepting of the whole idea.

The Petersons were simply elated! "Why, I'm getting the bestest little girl in the whole world as my very own daughter-in-law," Mr. Peterson stated. "I couldn't be any happier, Anna Louise. You guys have made our day!"

Carol Peterson then spoke. "Anna, you're going to make the best wife for my son that I could have ever dreamed or hoped for! You know that we have loved you since the very first time we met." A pause in the conversations occurred, in which everyone continued with their desserts, looking up occasionally at each other in excitement. Mrs. Peterson continued. "Margie, you know that I'll be more than willing to help you with anything you desire, so don't worry about a thing. Between you, me, and Amanda, we'll tackle this little obstacle and have that wedding set up in no time flat! Just say the word and we'll respond as needed."

"Thanks Carol," Margie Miller responded. "I know we will work well together and it will be the doggone best wedding that Fairaday, Georgia, has ever seen! Isn't it all just a bit too exciting, though?"

"Yes, it is," Joe Peterson said, "but we're going to have the best wedding ever. I would not be surprised if the whole town of Fairaday turns out for this one! Reverend Miller, do you think the Methodist Church will hold the entire town of Fairaday?"

Reverend John Henry Miller spoke up and said, "Well, we may have to restructure the building in some way in order to accomplish that great feat. Don't you think, ladies, that you will need to send out invitations for such a special event as this so there isn't a problem with overcrowding? If you simply open it up to anyone and everyone, I feel certain that there will be many disappointed folks who wouldn't be able to get into the church!" Reverend Miller had suggested that since Melody and Anna Louise had asked him to perform the ceremony, he would ask Reverend Leroy Jones at the Fairaday Baptist Church, Brad's pastor, to do the marriage counseling for Brad and Anna Louise, and he would do the counseling for Melody and Heath. Everyone agreed that that was an excellent idea. Brother Jones could share in the ceremonial duties with Reverend Miller, and it would truly be a community event in that respect!

Well, the little town of Fairaday was alive and buzzing with the news of the double wedding. The announcement appeared, not on the society page, but on the FRONT PAGE of the weekly Sentinel! It surprised everyone to see it there, but Larry Felding, the newspaper editor, felt that the news of the wedding was worthy of front-page coverage, after all, it was much more important than the local Fairaday sewer problems the city had been having! Felding had followed the lives of these kids since their birth and knew about the intricacies of their lives. He had followed Brad during his high school football career and had written great articles about him in the Sentinel. Furthermore, he knew all about Anna Louise's health conditions, her high school career, and her college career at the University of Georgia, Melody's graduation from Valdosta State, and the reputation of Reverend Miller in the community. All of these things added up to a fantastic front page story!

Chapter Twelve
Glorious Summertime!

Things rolled busily along in Fairaday during that summer. Anna Louise worked at Barden's Five-and-Dime while she awaited any news from Wake Forest about a potential job offer. The wedding plans were coming along fine, and she and Brad were in monthly sessions with the Reverend Leroy Jones at the Baptist church. They were discovering new and exciting things about one another as their love continued to grow. Melody received word that she would be teaching third grade at Tompkin's Elementary in the fall. Just what she had wanted! Her classroom would be two doors down the hall from Mrs. Miller's room. Brad continued living in Mount Vernon for the time being, and pastored the small Baptist church out in the country. Oak Grove Baptist was very proud to have a young man of his caliber and would certainly hate to see him go when August rolled around.

In late July, Anna Louise received a call from Wake Forest about a position that was available in a local nursing home chain headquartered in Wake Forest. They wanted her to work with recovering stroke victims in helping them to re-establish their speech. She would be shared with three different nursing homes in the area on a rotating basis. The job would pay a little over $30,000 to start, which would certainly help her and Brad through the tough times of seminary for the next three years. Without even thinking twice about it, she promised the advisor that she would be in Wake Forest the very next Monday to interview for the position. She would ask Brad if he could drive her up there for the meeting.

Anna Louise impressed the nursing home officials so much that they immediately hired her on the spot! She would begin work on September 15th, five days after their wedding. Brad took Anna Louise by the little two-bedroom apartment they would be living in in September, and her heart was filled with an unspeakable joy when she saw it! Little flower beds out front on either side of the entrance; ivy covered doorway; quaint little cul-de-sac, with their apartment at the end of the street. It was a dream come true for her. She hugged Brad, as they started to leave, and assured him that it was the most beautiful little place imaginable! All of a sudden, Anna Louise noticed something as they were turning away from the apartment to head back to the car. Brad asked her what was wrong and Anna Louise said, "Brad, look over the entrance and tell me what you see."

Brad responded, "What is it Anna Louise? I can't

read your mind. I see a roof with shingles and a couple of windows and a front door."

"No, no, no!" Anna replied. Look at those numbers . . . the house numbers. What are they?"

"It says 9-1-0 for goodness sake! What is so mysterious about that, Anna Louise?" It had not dawned on Brad at that moment the significance of those numbers until Anna Louise pointed it out.

"Honey, those numbers represent our wedding date, 9/10! Isn't that amazing? I can hardly believe it, but you've found the ideal apartment, in an ideal neighborhood, with the ideal number engraved on the door! Now tell me that's just a coincidence!"

"Sweetheart, I'm sorry for being so blind. That is truly amazing, but something even more amazing than that is YOU! I love you with all of my heart and am looking forward to living with you for the rest of my life." Brad embraced her right there on the sidewalk near their car. Things couldn't be any better, Anna Louise thought to herself.

On their way back to Mount Vernon, they were ceaselessly involved in conversations about the future, the wedding, their jobs, and their prospects for Brad to receive a church near Wake Forest. God had really answered every prayer in their lives to this point, and life was good. Seems that all of the right choices were being made, and the future was certainly bright with endless possibilities.

The wedding would not only be a DOUBLE ceremony, but would be officiated by two of the areas most admired ministers – Reverend Leroy Jones of Fairaday Baptist and Reverend John Henry Miller of Fairaday United Methodist. It would be referred to around Fairaday as "the event" of the year! It was a gorgeous ceremony and detailed to every possible degree. Margie Miller, Carol Peterson, and Amanda Harper worked long hours and days to put together this momentous occasion. The fruits of their labors showed in grand fashion!

Jennifer Pittman, a good friend of Melody and Anna Louise, sang "Ave Maria" at the beginning of the ceremony, and then Reverend Miller broke down and started crying like a baby, fighting back to hold his tears. He stumbled through the vows with both couples, as the tears threatened him once again. Jason had been asked to escort his sister to the altar, and Harold Baker, Melody's twelfth grade English-Lit teacher and a dear friend of her father's, escorted Melody.

Reverend John Henry Miller's throat began to tighten the further he delved into the ceremony. He eventually turned the service over to Brother Leroy Jones to finish the pronouncement of the couples and to lead them through the Unity Candle lighting. John Miller stood there watching, as he thought back through the years to those earlier days in Anna Louise's life. There were those times that they were unsure as to how long the little blessing of God would live. It had been day-to-day during those most troubling of years. And now, here she was—larger than life itself—on the greatest day of her life, standing before her earthly father with thanks to her heavenly Father. God really does work in mysterious and wonderful ways, he thought.

Following the wedding, attended by well over 400 townspeople, Brad and Anna Louise headed off for Lookout Mountain, Tennessee, for their honeymoon, while Heath and Melody headed south to the beaches of Florida. Brad and Anna Louise would return in three days to pack everything for their trip to Wake Forest. Time now was of the essence, and they had to move quickly. Reverend Miller had already secured a large yellow Ryder truck for their move, and he would be taking a few days off from his ministerial duties in order to help the couple move into their apartment. Mrs. Miller would accompany them as well to Wake Forest in the truck with John and Jason.

Moving Day was both sad and happy in Fairaday as that yellow Ryder truck and its entourage followed through town, beyond the only redlight, past the high school and the Dairy Queen, and then up Highway 16 on their way to Wake Forest, North Carolina. People waved to them from the sidewalks, from their storefronts, at Mixson's Amoco. A little group of their high school friends were gathered in front of the Dairy Queen as they passed by. They were all waving farewell to two of Fairaday's most beloved citizens. The road ahead would be filled with impediments and opportunities, but they were finally together forever! Their friends at the Dairy Queen had made a large sign which they held up as the entourage passed by that read, "GOOD LUCK, GUYS! WE LOVE YOU!" in large bold letters.

Townspeople had been very generous to both couples. Each had received an entire bedroom suite from Harbinger's Furniture Store; dishes, pots, pans, silverware and such from the largest shower ever held in Fairaday, Georgia; and Anna's folks had thrown in a few odds and ends, including a sofa and end tables for both of their living rooms. Mrs. Harper had given Anna Louise one of the most precious gifts of all, however. It was a beautiful christening bonnet to be used for their first child's baptism (it could work for either a boy or girl). Anna Louise would treasure this handstitched masterpiece forever! What a thoughtful lady Mrs. Harper had always been to her.

The move went smoothly, but with one hitch. Near the North Carolina border with South Carolina, one of the tires on the rear of the Ryder truck blew out! Luckily, Brad and Anna were in their car and they drove into the next town to get a mechanic to come out and assist with changing the tire. It killed about three hours of their trip in the hot South Carolina sun, but they were able to continue their journey to Wake Forest. Reverend Miller was soaked to the bone from helping the mechanic change the tire! He was also exhausted, and so Jason offered to drive, and Reverend Miller gladly obliged him.

The day after they moved in, everyone finally said

their goodbyes and left the young couple alone in Wake Forest. The two drove out to the seminary that afternoon, for Brad had never shown the school to Anna Louise. He showed her the different buildings in which he would have classes, and they walked through the library, which was open already. She was impressed, and they were both excited. They walked by the chapel on campus and noticed that the doors were open, so they walked in and saw the most majestic looking church they had ever seen! They walked arm in arm down to the altar. No one else was apparently around, so they knelt at the altar and Brad took Anna Louise's hand and offered a prayer.

"Dear Heavenly Father, we thank you for our lives together. You have blessed us beyond compare, and we are deeply indebted to You for everything in our lives. We pray here today, as we two join our hearts in complete submission to You, that we offer ourselves to thee as living sacrifices in thy kingdom's work. Use us, we pray, and give us strong hearts to endure these times of being away from our families and friends. Here in this special place, we both dedicate ourselves to thee. Bless us we pray. Amen."

Anna Louise thought it to be the most special prayer she had ever heard uttered. Brad was truly a wonderful man of God, and she felt completely at ease with Brad as her minister *and* husband. Then the thought occurred to her that they were now REVEREND AND MRS. BRADLEY J. PETERSON. It had a beautiful ring to it, Anna Louise thought. Tomorrow morning, they would meet with a new congregation looking for a student pastor. Oak Grove Baptist Church had not had a minister in the pulpit for three months and had requested the chaplaincy program at Wake Forest to help them secure one. Brad had been suggested for the position by his counselor at Wake, Dr. Freeman Porter, professor of Old Testament History. After preaching a trial sermon that next morning, the deacons held a brief meeting in the back of the church and voted to accept Brad on-trial as their new pastor if he would accept. He promised them he would give them an answer the following day, after he and Anna Louise prayed about the situation. All the way home Anna Louise talked about how quaint and beautiful the little church was and how friendly the people seemed to be. There were approximately 80 in worship that morning with a number of teenagers and children, which was a good sign of potential growth. Brad was already convinced that it was God who had led him to the church and it was God's Will that he accept the invitation, yet, he had been told by Professor Porter as well as Reverend Miller never to accept a position on the spot. Let the people know that you were a man of prayer, and tell them that you will need to prayerfully consider the appointment before giving a final answer.

Early Monday morning, Brad called Lester Franks, the head Deacon at Oak Grove, and told him that he would be there in full force as their new pastor the following Sunday morning. Anna Louise was to be at her new job Monday morning at the Silverview Nursing Home at 8:00 AM sharp! She was really excited about it, and actually got there at 7:45 AM. She was taken to her office space where she spent a few moments in prayer before the Resident Manager came in to greet her and to go over the day's assignments. Lisa Cox would be her supervisor and was a dear soul of approximately sixty years of age, Anna Louise had guessed. Her voice was so sweet sounding, as she talked with Anna Louise, and she knew immediately-that she was going to get along well with Miss Cox.

Anna Louise's first day was spent going to all three nursing homes in the area that she would be affiliated with in her new position. She met twenty-two patients who were suffering with speech impediments from such atrocities as strokes, automobile accidents and the like. Her work was truly cut out for her, and she would find herself scheduling rounds between the three homes on a daily basis.

That next Sunday, Brad preached his heart out at the little Oak Grove Baptist Church. The people seemed to be eagerly taking in every word he offered. The altar call had practically everyone down front and praying. It seemed to go on forever, but soon came to an end, and the head Deacon then announced that a dinner in honor of the Petersons would be enjoyed by all in the fellowship hall. Anna Louise and Brad were pleasantly surprised! The people at Oak Grove were so loving and accepting of the couple and made both of them feel right at home. Little did they expect it, but the church women had planned a wedding shower for the two of them for the next Thursday night at the church. They really lavished the couple with great gift items and several gift certificates. They were blessed.

Anna Louise loved her job, working daily with stroke victims. She saw progress in the techniques and methods she had learned to use while at Georgia. She had so impressed the nursing home staffs at all three facilities that soon they began referring to her as Doctor Anna, a name she would come to cherish! At times, however, the nursing homes would depress her. The constant smell of urine was always present, infiltrating her clothing, and she would carry the smell home with her each day. She also dealt with death and dying almost daily. It saddened her heart to lose a resident, but she was learning to accept it as part of the territory.

Brad's first day of classes was on September 21st. He quickly became entrenched in his studies, sermon preparation, visitations to church members, establishing a new youth program at the church, and trying hard to balance everything in between. He and Anna Louise saw very little of each other, mostly in passing through the house from one room to another and at night. Sundays were treasured days for them as they took those leisurely afternoons to spend time alone together. The couple was

given every Fifth Sunday off from Brad's preaching responsibilities, and they would head home to Fairaday to
spend some time with the family. They would drop in to
see Melody and Heath and spend a couple of hours with
them before going to their parents. In December of that
first year, they learned that Melody was expecting her first
child. It would be due on July 14th. The following March
would bring about further changes.

Chapter Thirteen
Back to Work Again!

Herschel Moore was back working his route two days after Barney's funeral. He had decided that Barney would not have wanted him to just crawl up somewhere in a corner and die, so he made his decision and asked Mr. Haskins if it was alright to come back so soon. With his approval, he was back on his regular truck by Friday.

All along the route that first day, people showed their sympathies to Herschel. He thanked them and tried to keep his composure. Every time he would pass an old pickup truck, he would stare a little harder, and sometimes swore to himself that he saw Barney behind the wheel!

The following Tuesday, Herschel had veered on the edge of the highway to miss an oncoming vehicle which had crossed over into his lane. The Pepsi truck flipped over in the ditch and had emptied out the majority of its load. Herschel was unscathed. He tried to explain to Mr. Haskins that the other car was at fault and that he had done the best he could to avoid the accident. Mr. Haskins insisted, however, that he come off the route and work in the warehouse for awhile until he had regained his composure.

"Herschel, this is for your own good. I know that you only have another year or two before retirement. Let me help you out here. It's getting dangerous out there on the road, and I wouldn't want anything to happen to you. You're my best worker, and I depend heavily upon you and your leadership. Help these young boys out in warehouse for me, and I'll see whether you're ready for the truck route again in a few weeks." Old man Haskins was insistent in his request, and nothing that Herschel could say would change his mind. He had been wanting to put younger men on the routes for several years but just couldn't bring himself to tell Barney and Herschel of his intentions. Now that Barney was gone and Herschel had come near to death himself, he had more reason to take Herschel off the route.

Herschel Moore knew in his heart of hearts that he would probably never run his route again. He was nobody's fool and knew that this was the straw that broke the camel's back. At any rate, he didn't have the heart for the road any longer. His best buddy was now gone, so he busied himself each day, 8 to 5, in the warehouse keeping track of the young boys who worked back there. He trained the new boys in how to crate the drinks, stack them, retrieve them for the trucks, and to check for bad bottles. He made it each day the best that he could, but his heart was really no longer in his work. Besides, his aging body couldn't keep up the pace with these younger fellows in the plant. He would have to look for something else to do or just simply retire. He had enough money and could support Carla and his little Missy comfortably for many years to come.

Herschel struggled along for the next year and a half, before his retirement, and continued to make ends meet. He and Carla were very happy together, and little Missy was growing by leaps and bounds. She had started to kindergarten that year and was loving it. Carla had more quality time to spend on her housework, and also with Herschel. They were the love of his life, and his every waking moment at home was spent doing things with the two of them. They took many trips together and worked faithfully at the church on a lot of different projects. Even old Bennie, the Jew across the street, would come over and spend more time with Herschel. He had actually become a good friend, although his card playing was still suspect. He started counting down the days before his retirement on September 15th of that year. Everyone joked about his retirement from the plant and kept asking what he planned to do. He had no earthly idea, he would tell them, and let it go at that.

Two weeks before his retirement, old man Haskins asked Herschel if he could deliver a couple of drink canisters up to Fitzgerald for their Friday night football game. These were the metal tanks that held the carbonated beverage, and Fitzgerald High had called saying they were short two canisters. Mr. Haskins told Herschel that he could be up there and back to Simpson by three o'clock that afternoon, and then he could just go home early if he would make that run. He would be taking the canisters in the company pickup which he had driven on numerous occasions around town the last year and a half, running errands for the boss.

Herschel agreed to go to Fitzgerald, so he loaded the two canisters in the back and headed out. It was a gorgeous day! Not a cloud in the sky. One of those surreal September afternoons that warmed the soul. Herschel could use the driving time to think about Carla, Missy, and himself and their future, if there really was one for him. He had often wondered what he was now capable of doing in these waning years of life, but he came up with no answers. He swore to himself, at one point along the journey, that he heard old Barney calling out to him. All of a sudden it came back to him. As he stood on the banks of Statham's Creek with the Civil Defense workers while they grappled for a body, he had turned to look for Barney's truck. He remembered then having seen the shadow of a person walking off in the distance toward Barney's old pickup and crawling up into the cab. He remembered the person waving a hand in the air as he jumped in the truck. Herschel felt shivers crawl all over his body as it dawned on him that it was probably old Barney's spirit rising from the murky waters of Statham's Creek and returning to his truck!

"I miss you, Buddy," he muttered to himself. "Never thought I'd ever miss someone as much as I miss you. I could really use you here with me right now if you could see fit to come down from heaven or wherever you are.

The road to Fitzgerald led him down State Highway 92 directly into town. Herschel used to deliver drinks to all of the businesses in Fitzgerald, but had not been there in a number of years since Barney had been given that route. Another place, another time, and it would have been Barney delivering those canisters that Friday afternoon. Herschel thought about all those things while he enjoyed the smooth journey. He thought back about sweet Elizabeth, the love of his life, and how miserable he had been since her departure. He lamented over the death of his dear friend, Barney, and how life had sunken to a new all time low since his departure, and how Carla and Missy were God's wonderful new gift to him. They had brought new meaning and purpose into his life and had gotten him back on the straight-and-narrow way. He had been carrying flowers to Barney's grave every Sunday since his burial. He didn't know why, but he had done it; just seemed like the right thing to do. Of course, Carla and Missy always accompanied him to that grave. That person in it would always be held special and dear to their hearts!

The afternoon sun danced and skipped over the highway as it passed through the tall pine trees on either side of the road. As Herschel crossed the bridge over the Cataluchie River, he sensed a strange feeling coming over him which he had never felt before. It almost took his breath away. Something inside of him just emptied, like some kind of evil, and he felt this warm, peaceful feeling all over.

Topping the hill beyond the river, Herschel was suddenly blinded by the brilliant afternoon sun beaming through the windshield. Alone, with his various thoughts and the evening sun shining in brightly, he looked up and saw nothing but a warm brightness ahead near Crookman's Hill. That's the last thing he remembered before it happened.

Chapter Fourteen
The Bishop Calls!

In early March, Reverend Miller received a telephone call from Bishop Richard Rollins in Macon. The Bishop requested a meeting between the two for the following afternoon. Reverend Miller had no possible idea of what the meeting was about, but he accepted the Bishop's invitation and drove to Macon to meet with him. Upon seeing the Bishop, he learned that the Bishop and cabinet had desires to move the Millers to a new appointment in June to historic Mulberry United Methodist Church in Macon. The congregation at Mulberry was asking specifically for the Millers, and the Bishop felt that it was the right move at the right time for them. He urged Reverend Miller to accept the move. The congregation was approximately 2,000 in membership and would afford Reverend Miller the opportunity of working with an extended staff, the first of his ministry. He would be absolutely foolish to turn down such a wonderful opportunity but would be saddened beyond belief to leave the town that had given birth to his children and had nurtured them through the toughest times and most blessed times of their lives. They had given twenty years of their lives in service to the best little community in Georgia. It would be a most difficult thing to do, but he guessed that the Bishop was right. He would call the following morning and announce to the Bishop his desires to take the appointment, after going home to pray with Margie. The Bishop agreed to come to Fairaday the following Sunday to make the official announcement to Reverend Miller's congregation, and to preach the sermon as well. He felt that it would help soothe the people if their Bishop actually came down to Fairaday and made this announcement himself. It would have been much harder for Reverend Miller to have made such an announcement to his people.

Margie Miller was excited about their move, although she would miss her co-workers of twenty years at Tompkins Elementary School. She knew Macon, a larger city about two hours from Fairaday, would afford them everything they needed and that John wouldn't have to travel so extensively to area hospitals to see his parishioners because Macon had three major hospitals within the city proper. Margie had always taken the moving process with ease and excitement, whereas John had labored over each move as if in the grieving process of losing a loved one.

Although packing up a house that had been kept for twenty years was very unappealing to Margie, she knew that it would probably be best for them in the long run. Jason would soon be graduating from Valdosta State and was a very independent young man, so she didn't worry about him. Anna Louise and Brad were set in Wake Forest for the next three or four years at least, so the doors had been opened for a move, and she felt the hand of God was in it. There was really nothing at this point to hold them back. Besides, if the Bishop recommended the move for John, then they should take his advice and make the change. It would give another ministerial family the opportunity to move to Fairaday and to be blessed by such a wonderful congregation and town. Sure, they would have regrets, but you always have them no matter what you do in life. You'll always wonder WHAT IF? Would things really have been different if they stayed? Life is always about choices. Sometimes, fate has its own way as well.

The move came on the second Wednesday of June that year. Two moving vans arrived early that morning and crews packed everything in the Miller household and took it to their new parsonage in Macon, where they began the unloading process. The Fairaday townsfolk came by in numbers to wish the Millers well in their new appointment and knew that Brother John would be very successful there. After all, he had taken a congregation of approximately 125 and had turned it into well over a thousand strong in the past twenty years! The Fairaday United Methodist Church had become an example to other ministers in the area, and Brother John was asked frequently to speak at district and conference events. His popularity had grown, and he was in great demand.

Margie walked into the new parsonage in Macon

and was very impressed with how beautiful it was. It was well-appointed from top to bottom. She was having one of her hissy fits, immediately trying to figure out where to put the things they had brought with them from Fairaday. The new parsonage had everything they needed, so a lot of the Miller goods would have to be stored somewhere. Reverend John would have to rent one of those storage buildings in town in which to keep all of their excess baggage.

John's first Sunday at Mulberry was simply fantastic, as well as nerve wracking! The church had two morning services. There were over 350 people at the early 9:30 AM service, and a collective 655 at the 11 AM service. Pastor Miller had never preached to that many people in any ONE month of Sundays before! Wow! Was he going to have a great time there, he thought. He had an Associate Minister who conducted the music, one for the Children's Church and ministries, one for the Youth ministries, a Lay Leader who conducted the Order of Worship, and wonderful choirs at both services. The 11:00 AM service was carried over the local Macon TV station so his sermons would have to be well-prepared, he thought. When the Pastor Parish Relations Committee met with John the first week, they had insisted that his main responsibility and duty would be to PREACH the Word! He would be keeping "regular" hours each day at the church study for the first time in his ministry. In each of his other five pastorates, Reverend Miller had to do it all! He had even led the choir in an earlier appointment. Finally, he thought, he would be freed from so many responsibilities in order to concentrate on his sermons. He liked this new position even better now!

Fifth Sundays had to be split now for Brad and Anna Louise between Fairaday, with Brad's parents, Melody and Heath, and Macon with the Millers. It made it a bit tougher on Brad and Anna Louise, but they managed. In late November, Brad was asked by the Wake Forest Chaplain to consider taking the position of Assistant Chaplain for the college. This was quite an honor for Brad and carried an annual stipend of $10,000. That would help them tremendously and would allow him to preach at Oak Grove on Sundays as well. His main responsibility at Wake Forest would be conducting Wednesday evening vespers and would be available to counsel with students as needed. Anna Louise was very proud of Brad and agreed with his taking this extra duty.

Chapter Fifteen
A Child is Born

The following spring, wonderful news spread across Georgia like a summer wildfire. Anna Louise was going to have a baby. Everyone seemed pleased except Margie Miller. Always the skeptic and overly concerned mother, Margie was still living in the past with the old fears of the leukemia, the treatments, all of the pain and suffering that had come with the disease. She had a difficult time understanding WHY Anna Louise would allow herself to become pregnant, knowing all the while that the child could be a receptor of the same dreaded disease.

"Honey, I'm afraid for Anna Louise," Margie said to Pastor John one day after having received the news. "You know our little girl is so frail and has been through so much in her life. What if she can't have the baby? What if . . ."

Pastor Miller cut her off short. "Margie, for God's sake, accept what has happened to our little girl and be happy for her. We'll take whatever consequences life throws at us, just like you and I did when she was born. This should be a very happy occasion for Brad and Anna Louise, and I will not allow you to spoil it. Don't throw a damper into the situation. Let's just be thankful again that God has sent His blessings upon us."

"I know. I know, honey. I'm just scared for her. I guess I just need to place everything in God's hands and allow His will to be done. I just can't help, though, to be overly concerned." Margie was very sympathetic in her last response.

"That's understandable, dear, but please try not to let it show when they come this weekend. Let's rejoice and celebrate with them and let them know how happy we are for the both of them.

"I will. I promise. I won't mention a thing about it," Margie replied, with resolve.

The weekend finally arrived following the news, and they could both hardly wait for Brad and Anna Louise to arrive in Macon. They would spend most of the day on Saturday in Fairaday with the Petersons, with Melody and Heath, and arrive on Sunday morning to spend most of the day in church with the Millers. They would have lunch together with the Millers and visit a short while in the afternoon, before heading back to Wake Forest. The trips would become less and less as Anna Louise progressed in her pregnancy, because of the strain of traveling such a long distance. Jason was away from Valdosta State down in Florida for a weekend baseball series with two different colleges and wouldn't be in Macon for the reunion. Jason really didn't like Macon that much and he would only stay on a given weekend with his parents for part of a day and then travel down to Fairaday to spend the rest of the weekend with some of his old high school buddies. As of late, Jason had been dating a beautiful young girl from Key West, Florida, who also attended Valdosta State. She was truly a peach and had the sweetest disposition. Occasionally, Jason would bring her to Macon to visit with his parents. The Millers had been very impressed with her academics and had accepted Jason's choice. Nothing serious at this point, but they were seeing a lot of each other, especially now that the Millers had moved so far north.

"Mom, Dad, we hope you're both happy for us," Anna Louise said before she could even get out of the car in the driveway at the parsonage in Macon.

"Oh, honey," Margie said, "Get out of that car and come to me! I am so very happy for you, dear, and can't wait. When is the baby due? Have you found a gynecologist and obstetrician in Wake Forest yet? Are you going to use the Lamaze method of childbirth?" Margie simply bombarded Anna Louise with questions that even she had not considered at this early point in the pregnancy.

"Calm down, Margie," Pastor Miller jumped in. "Give the girl a breather! They've just spent the last six hours on the road, and I'm sure they're very tired and worn to a frazzle. Give them a chance to come inside before all the questions pop out."

"I'm sorry, dear. I just can't wait to find out about everything. You know how I am." Margie was eager in her attempt to learn as much as possible about the pregnancy. Her enthusiasm was evident.

As the couples shared a wonderful weekend together, both families celebrated the good news. It was a sad moment for all concerned when Anna Louise and Brad pulled out of the driveway that Sunday afternoon and headed back to Wake Forest. But they would be back again soon. They had promised.

Chapter Sixteen
Raymond Carter and Roscoe Seckinger

Raymond Carter had been working with the county forestry department for twenty-seven years. He loved his work and was Chief Ranger. He enjoyed the outdoors and was an avid hunter. He was known around these parts as a sort of Davy Crockett or Daniel Boone, always learning new ways to do old things and to improve upon them. He could zero in on a deer from 150 yards away without a scope and down the rascal in a heartbeat! He was that precise in everything he did. His wife Frances was often perturbed with him because he seemed to stay in the woods more often than at home. She had her own life, however, and spent most of her time in Tifton or Fitzgerald shopping with her friends.

"Raymond, don't forget to pick up the lunch I made you on the counter before you leave," Frances shouted across the house when she heard Raymond walking through on his way out. "Made you a couple of sandwiches and put a can of sardines in there as well."

"Thank you, Honey. I appreciate that. We've got a big job burning off the woods over in Tift County today. We're going to help their department since the area covers a wide expanse of trees." Raymond's voice trailed as he left through the front door, got into his forestry truck, and headed to work.

Raymond had been leaving a bit early lately because he was stopping in at Earline's Diner for coffee with the boys. They had a whale of a time catching up on all of the latest news around Simpson and Collier County. That's where Raymond began picking up a lot of his tall tales. Roscoe Seckinger was the chief architect of most of those tall tales and was Raymond's best friend and co-worker. Roscoe was the best worker in the field that Raymond had ever encountered. They hunted practically every Saturday together, even if it wasn't hunting season, for a particular prey. They just enjoyed each others' company and being out in the wilderness together. They also did a lot of fishing, and Roscoe had just recently landed a largemouth bass that nearly took the old record. It weighed 18 pounds and 6 ounces. The record, he remembered, was 22.4 pounds and was caught by a young 19 year old farm boy by the name of George Washington Perry. He actually caught the fish about 50 miles away from Simpson near Jacksonville, Georgia. It had been caught in Montgomery Lake, a slough off the Ocmulgee River. The Cataluchie River ran into the Ocmulgee, so that's where Raymond and Roscoe usually went fishing.

They had their own John boats and every type of lure you could imagine in their tackle boxes. If they didn't have it, well, it just didn't exist!

Roscoe had caught the big lunker two weeks ago near the Cataluchie River Bridge, about 30 yards or so down river. At first, he thought he had snagged a huge old black catfish, but then it started jumping out of the water as Roscoe would pull and reel, pull and reel, until he could see the eyes and figure of the giant. Biggest fish he had ever landed, so he took it into Simpson to have it weighed at Siler's Feed Mill. They had some of those Morse Scales there that were supposed to be very precise; and Roscoe knew that this monster might tip the scales in his favor.

James Siler ran the Feed Mill and welcomed Roscoe that Saturday afternoon as he walked into the office. "What ya got today, Roscoe? Never know what you gone bring in here for me to weigh. Got another deer in the truck? You know it ain't deer season, don't you?" James always shot the breeze with Roscoe whenever they got together.

"Why, you old rascal, I got a bona fide world record bass out there in the back of my pickup! Caught 'em this morning on the Cataluchie and it took me two hours to land him on the bank!" Roscoe's tales grew the more he talked. "In fact, I caught him on just some red wigglers and a hook. Want you to weigh him for me, Jimmy." Everybody called James "Jimmy" in these parts. In fact, if you called him James, that was a sure sign that you didn't know him.

"Roscoe, bring him in. Let's see if he can top the scales at 10 pounds! Bet he ain't even that big, but for your satisfaction, I'll weigh him for you." With that having been said, Roscoe went back to the truck and took out the string of fish he had caught that morning in the river. Jimmy looked out the office window and couldn't believe his eyes! Why, that fish dangled almost to the ground as Roscoe walked, holding tightly onto the fish string! Maybe he did have a record-breaker. Jimmy called Henry Simmons down at Simpson's Bar and asked him to come down there as a witness.

"Henry, I think old Roscoe has caught the new world's record bass. Better get down here right now and witness the weigh-in with us." Jimmy was getting a bit excited at this point and wanted to make sure that someone other than he and Roscoe witnessed the weigh-in.

"Alright, Jimmy. Ain't nobody here in the bar right now, so I'll lock up and be right there."

Roscoe walked into the office with his string of fish and Jimmy immediately led him back outside. "Get them damn smelly fish out of my office, Roscoe. You know better than that. Just had it vacuumed and cleaned yesterday. We'll weigh him out yonder at the crib on the Morse Scales. That'll be much more accurate than these here in the office."

"Boy, I tell you, you are one of the most curious people I've ever known, Jimmy. You is somethin' else!" Roscoe coddled with Jimmy like this all the time.

"Alright, get that thing off the stringer and hand him to me," Jimmy said as he set up the scales. "I'm guessing maybe 12 pounds, Roscoe. What ya think?"

"Ah, Jimmy, you know that fish is gonna weigh more than that! You want to make a bet on it?" Roscoe asked.

"Yea, I'll bet you $20 that that fish ain't any heavier than 12 pounds!"

"You got yourself a deal, Jimmy." Roscoe almost shouted. "Gonna make me $20 bucks today and set a new world's record."

"You old fool," Jimmy said, as he looked at Roscoe handing him the fish. "You always think you've got the world's record buck, the world's record catfish, and now you think you've got the world's record bass! How stupid can one guy be, Roscoe? Haven't they taught you anything at that forestry department?"

Henry Simmons drove up at that point and got out of his car and walked over to the scales, eyeing the big fish as he approached. "Dang it, Roscoe, you gotta a record fish there, I do believe! Where'd you catch him?"

Roscoe told Henry and Jimmy, "Ain't none of your business. Would you be willing to tell your customers at the bar exactly how much you had to pay for a bottle of whiskey? No! That's your trade secret. I gotta keep my secret too because everybody within a hundred miles of here would start fishin' my hole!"

Jimmy took the huge fish and placed it on a metal tray that he had already weighed for the difference (2 pounds and 6 ounces) and then placed the tray and fish on the Morse Scales. All eyes were on the scales as they tilted back and forth for what seemed like an eternity for Roscoe and finally settling on the exact figure of 21 pounds and 2 ounces! "Looks like you didn't break the record, Roscoe," Jimmy said. "By my calculations, it weighs 18 pounds and 6 ounces."

"Well, shoot!" Roscoe said. "I really thought this was the one. You know that Field and Stream Magazine is offering nearly 5 million dollars to the person who can catch the new record Large Mouth Bass! Boy, was I a hopin' for that!"

"Sorry, Roscoe," Henry Simmons piped in. "Guess you won't get rich today!"

"Well, I don't know 'bout that cause Jimmy and I had a bet of $20. Jimmy said it wouldn't weigh a hair over 12 pounds! Well, he was wrong, so I guess you owe me $20 bucks, Jimmy."

"Wait a minute, Roscoe. I didn't tell you how much it was gonna cost you for me to use my scales on this fish, did I? You didn't ask, but I've gotta charge you for my time and labor!" Jimmy jokingly said to Roscoe.

"You stinkin' belly-whopper, you ain't gonna charge me anything! For all the stuff I've done for you out on your farm in my off-time, you ain't gonna tell me now that I owe you for weighing a stinkin' fish, are you?" Roscoe's voice had a hint of anger in it as he stared at Jimmy.

Jimmy reached into his back pocket and took a twenty out of his billfold and handed it to Roscoe. "You a hard fellow to bargain with Roscoe. What you gonna do now with that fish?"

"Gone take him up by the newspaper office and let 'em take a picture of it. That's what I'm gone do. Then everybody 'round here will remember old Roscoe's Bass." He was proud of his catch, even if it didn't break the record. It was much larger than anyone else's catch had been in this area for a long time.

When Roscoe got home with his fish, his wife Mabelline took it out back and cleaned it and prepared it for supper. Roscoe called Raymond and his wife to invite them over for fish and told Raymond all about his catch. Raymond was really proud of his buddy but was disappointed that he hadn't brought it by for him to see before he saw it all fried-up on a plate!

That Monday morning Roscoe and Raymond drove the Forestry truck to Tifton to help out with Tift County's fire crew in the burning of that large spread of pine trees. They always enjoyed working with the boys from Tifton and would often share heavy jobs like this one.

About three o'clock in the evening, they got a call on their C.B. radio to respond to a car crash over on highway 92 near the Cataluchie River Bridge. The dispatcher said that one of the vehicles was on fire and sitting in the middle of the road near Crookman's Hill. They jumped into their truck, which carried a tank of water on the back, and headed up highway 92 to the wreck. When they got there, cars were parked on both sides of the road everywhere. Whenever there's a wreck out in the countryside, the Forestry Department is called to help with the recovery process, and most particularly if there's a fire involved that could ignite neighboring woods.

"My God!" Roscoe started, as they gazed up ahead at the site. "Boy, this is a rough one, Raymond. We better hurry. I ain't seen a wreck this bad in a long time."

"Guess we're gonna need the pumper to come out from the office on this one," Raymond stated. "It'll take us probably a couple hours to put this out!"

"Wonder who it might be, Raymond?" Roscoe said as they pulled up and blocked the hillside from other traffic passing through. Raymond grabbed the hose from the tank on the back and cranked up the engine to pump the water to the car which was on fire, straddling the highway sideways.

"My God! There's no telling, Roscoe. This is a bad one. This one's bad." Raymond's voice was chill and hasty as he ran with the hose towards the car which was on fire.

Chapter Seventeen
The Babies Arrive!

Melody was due in July and Anna Louise in November. Both would come in the same year, both would be very beautiful and healthy. They would share the same birth-year as their mothers' had shared. Melody had a 6 pound 8 ounce baby girl and named her Stephanie Ann. Anna Louise had a boy, 5 pound 10 ounces and named him Bradley Scott Peterson. Both mothers' lives were now changing rapidly, and there didn't seem to be much time for Brad, Anna Louise, and Bradley to return home to Georgia as frequently as before, so the Millers and Petersons would carpool to Wake Forest together whenever the opportunity arose. They were all very excited about little Bradley and made numerous trips to Wake Forest to see their little family in that first year.

At the end of Brad's second year of a three year seminary track, he began his clinical pastoral education work at Wake Forest University Baptist Medical Center. He was to complete this work on a daily basis, Monday through Friday, which put a great strain on him to carry out his other duties with the chaplaincy program and his little Oak Grove Church responsibilities. The folks at Oak Grove had been very gracious to him and Anna Louise and allowed him freedom to do whatever he needed to do at the University. Brad could not have asked for a better congregation.

Brad's CPE (Clinical Pastoral Education) work dealt with the ICU (Intensive Care Unit) patients. It would be his responsibility to visit the ICU each afternoon and converse with each of the patients, most particularly with the ones who had requested a chaplain. He would also contact local area ministers and inform them of a church member who was in the unit. Three hours of work each evening became a draining experience for Brad, but he persevered. Little Bradley needed a Dad at home as well, and Anna Louise was very stressed knowing that she would have to go back to her speech therapy job after her maternity leave was up. They had looked at several day care centers in the immediate area and had settled on Little Angels, only four blocks from their apartment. Little Angels seemed to have the best facilities and the warmest workers of all the centers they had visited. Anna Louise was just hesitant to leave little Bradley after only two months with him, but she began to realize it was necessary.

Brad's first day of CPE was quite enlightening. He encountered a young 16 year-old boy who had been in a tragic car wreck with 6 other youth. Four of them were instantly killed at the site and another was on the second floor at the hospital in fair condition. Tommy Barton, the 16 year-old, had been the driver of the vehicle and was suffering from guilt and a very badly bruised and battered body. Tubes were everywhere! Tommy was in and out of consciousness, and Brad walked in and reached for Tommy's hand.

"Hello, Tommy, I'm Chaplain Peterson, and I've been assigned to work with you over the next three months or as long as you are here. I just want you to know that should you need anything, I will do my very best to get it for you. Mostly, my role will be in helping you to cope with your injuries and to help you understand what has happened and how you wound up here in ICU." Brad was tender with his words and noticed that Tommy was coming and going while he spoke. Finally, Tommy's eyes opened and Brad had a startling response.

"What the hell do you want, preacher? Do you know that I am responsible for killing four of my closest friends, my girlfriend included? Do you know that I was the one driving and that I can never live that down! What you can do for me right now is to tell the nurses to give me something that will take my life. I don't want to live. How could I ever face the parents of those four kids?" Tommy was stammering out the words, but with much anger in them.

"Tommy, I know this is all tragic, but you've got to come to terms with it. If you are responsible for the other four lives, then you need to wake up and live in a new and more responsible fashion in place of their existence. You cannot simply go away as though nothing happened. You have to find the strength deep inside yourself to pull out of this thing, and I want you to know that I'm here to help you and so is God." Brad was heavy hearted at this point and struggled for the right words to say.

"God is not my friend! If he was, then why would he let my friends die in the wreck? Just ain't right. I tried . . ." Tommy was gasping for breath and Brad asked him to just slow down and take his time. "I tried to bring the car back from the edge of the road but it started flipping over and over. That tractor-trailer ran us off the road. Damn his soul in an eternity of Hell!"

"Tommy, the wreck wasn't God's fault. It was a simple act of fate. The truck driver was in the wrong and had fallen asleep at the wheel. That's the testimony he gave to the authorities. The wreck wasn't your fault! You need to realize that and allow me to help you through the process of recovery. O.K.? Listen, I've got to go but I'll be back to see you again tomorrow. You just think about all that we've discussed and maybe we can continue our conversation tomorrow evening." Brad was finding the words easier and easier to say. He knew that the hand of God had to be upon him at this point and began to realize what the CPE program was trying to accomplish for all ministerial candidates. It pushes a person beyond their faith in extreme situations where they have to strive for answers to some very complex issues in life. It's simple to preach a sermon on Sunday morning, but what would that same preacher do if he was called in the middle of the night to the hospital and found one of his parishioners dying on a gurney in the emergency room? What would he say to that dying person? How would he respond?

Or what about a young mother who just delivered a still-born child? What would you say to her? How could you make it better? Could you lead her back from the threshold to a more meaningful life?

Day two at University Baptist Medical Center found Brad walking across the battery of the ICU toward Tommy's room. Nurse Fielding caught Brad's sleeve and stopped him in mid-step.

"Brad, just wanted to let you know that Tommy passed at 11:30 PM last night. He had a massive aneurism and there was nothing anyone could do to save him. I am so sorry because I know how long you spent with him yesterday." Nurse Fielding was so sympathetic in her tone of voice.

"I can't believe it, Nurse Fielding. I thought he was going to make it. He was beginning to talk more to me and showed signs of recovery." Brad expressed his broken heart over the matter, and Nurse Fielding knew it.

"I'm sorry, Honey," she replied, "but these things happen around here all the time. Our saying is that you have to strike while the pan is hot! Things change around here very quickly, and what you might consider is not life threatening, all of a sudden becomes so. That's life in the ICU. Welcome to the family, Son." Nurse Fielding was trying her best to encourage Brad to move forward with his work. There were other people to deal with. "Would you go over to Bed 9 and visit with Clarice Davis for me, sweetie? She's been in here now for about two months. Eighty-two years old and dying of congestive heart failure. She coded on us twice last night. We were successful in bringing her back both times, but she could go at any minute!"

"Wow!" Brad thought to himself. "This is going to be the most difficult job I've ever had. I would much rather be back on my uncle's farm loading watermelons any day than having to deal with this. What am I going to say to an eighty-two year old lady that will give her hope or help her to die in a respectful fashion?"

Brad stood outside of Clarice Davis's room and looked in at her. She had tubes and monitors hooked up all around her and made a faint wheezing sound, almost undetectable. He slowly moved into the room, careful not to disturb any of the medical equipment in the process. As he neared her bed, he could see that her eyes had been following him.

"May I help you, son?" Mrs. Davis asked.

"Mrs. Davis, my name is Brad Peterson and I have been assigned to your case as chaplain. I have just dropped in to see how you're doing." Brad responded.

"I'm fine, young man, but how are you?" she asked.

Brad couldn't believe that the lady was actually asking *him* how he was doing when she was the one in such terrible condition! Mrs. Davis began coughing, and Brad asked her if she would prefer that he return later.

"Son, I'm not sure that I'll be around here later. You best make your peace now while you can, and then get on with your business." Her voice was soft and sweet as she spoke to Brad.

"Ma'am, I was wondering if I could help you in some way." Brad gently asked.

"Son, I'm really beyond the realm of 'Help'. Last night I nearly died, and I'm ready to die, but these people just won't let me. My body is tired; I've been weary for the longest since Carl left me six years ago, and I just don't have anything left to live for. It's sad to get into this condition, I know, but for what earthly reason would I want to go on living?" Her statements burned into Brad like a fire. What could he possibly say in return that would make a difference in her life at this stage?

"Mrs. Davis, we never know the full Will of God for our lives, nor why He leaves us here on this earth when all of our friends and loved ones around us have gone. But I would suspect that there are people in your life who are still around who love you and are concerned about you. Am I right?" Brad asked.

"Son, you're pretty observant. Indeed I have! I have a wonderful son who works at the Trust Bank right here in Wake Forest, and he has two beautiful children who are the lights of my life. Carl and Becky are so good to me. They usually come by during visiting hours just to check on me. Why, I've actually left everything in their names when I die." She spoke with conviction as Brad took it all in.

"I'm sure, Mrs. Davis, that Carl and Becky would much rather have you alive than any of your other possessions. Dying is a very sacred act when it is done in God's timing. We should not begrudge that holy moment when our Lord returns for us, but we should do our best at all times until he comes." Brad had just instructed a lady almost four times his own age! He nervously awaited her response.

"Young man, certainly you are wise beyond your age, and I do appreciate what you are saying. I thank you sincerely for coming in and trying to cheer up my day. Fact is, I cannot do anything for myself. I'm worthless and useless around here and just want to go home," she stated.

"I know, Mrs. Davis, but then I wouldn't have anyone to talk to. I feel the need for us to have a prayer together, if that's O.K. with you."

"Fire away, chaplain! I've been needin' a good prayer. Let's see what you've got." The challenge was now before him. He remembered a brief prayer in his prayer book, which he carried with him, written by John Donne and so he read it at that moment for Mrs. Davis.

"Bring us, O Lord God, at our last awakening, into the house and gate of heaven, to enter into that gate, and dwell in that house where there shall be no darkness nor dazzling, but one equal light; no noise nor silence, but one equal music; no fears nor hopes, but one equal possession; no ends nor beginnings, but one equal eternity; in the habitation of thy glory and dominion, world without end. Amen."

Brad placed his hand upon Mrs. Davis' hand while he prayed this prayer. He could feel the warmth flow throughout his being and knew that she would receive it faithfully.

"Young man, that was absolutely beautiful and so meaningful. It was exactly what I needed. Will you come back again?" Mrs. Davis asked.

"Yes, you bet. I'll be back again tomorrow evening about this same time. You hold tight, but if something happens, I'll know where you are." Brad knew the words had to be coming directly from God for he had never had such insight in his life.

The relationship with Mrs. Davis continued for a couple of more weeks, and then she was moved down to another floor in the hospital. Her grandchildren were wonderful and had met a few times with Brad, and he felt that she was making a very positive recovery. That beautiful prayer perhaps gave her a new lease on life. Strange, isn't it, how something so short and succinct can really serve to turn our lives around!

Anna Louise was groping daily to pour herself back into her job at the three nursing homes, but now the tasks were arduous. Every moment seemed to be filled with little Bradley. She could hardly wait to get home to him. In the first couple of weeks back at work, she found herself overly anxious and constantly looking at the clock for 5:00 PM to roll around. She needed Bradley as much as he needed her. It is very difficult to separate a new born from its mother, and for Anna Louise, an eight hour day was an eternity.

Mulberry United Methodist Church in Macon was continuing to grow rapidly under Reverend John Henry Miller's able leadership. Margie had taken a year off after they moved there, became completely bored, and then returned to the classroom again at Perkins Elementary teaching fourth grade. This wasn't particularly her choice, but she would make the most of it. She really liked the school she was appointed to, which happened to be a science and math magnet school. These were her two strongest areas of concentration in college, so now she would be given the opportunity of concentrating on them in this magnet school setting. She immediately became friends with her other peers at the school. There were six other teachers at Perkins who attended church at Mulberry, so Margie began to feel right at home. They were all very helpful to her and had her indoctrinated in a hurry. Starting over, she thought, isn't so bad after all! She had finally found a new home.

In May of Brad's year of graduation from Wake Forest, he was invited to speak at First Baptist Church in McRae, Georgia, about an hour and a half from Macon. It was a nice little town with antebellum styled homes along main street. The church was very warm and receptive that

Sunday and decided to meet with Brad and Anna Louise in mid-afternoon to discuss the possibilities of their accepting the call to pastor First Baptist. The Millers took the Sunday off and met Brad and Anna Louise at the morning worship service. Reverend Miller sat in awe as he listened to a very well constructed sermon given by his son-in-law. This was actually the first time he had ever heard Brad preach! Margie was happy because she was able to keep little Bradley and hold him in her arms during the service. He never made a peep! He was a good baby and was the reflection of Anna Louise and Brad's love. Although serving double-duty holding the child and listening to Brad, she never missed a single word he said. She was amazed at his ability.

Brad and Anna Louise met with the committee at 3:00 PM that afternoon. They offered the pulpit unanimously to Brad, but he refused to give them an answer at that time. It would only come later after he and Anna Louise prayerfully considered the Lord's Will for their lives. They left the committee with the understanding that Brad would contact them in a few days with his answer. Having the opportunity to be close to her mother and father again and only a couple of hours from Melody, Heath, Jason and Fairaday, Anna Louise was ready to start packing!

Following the interview, Brad and Anna Louise and little Bradley followed the Millers back to the parsonage in Macon where they would spend the next couple of days, both having secured days off from their respective jobs. Brad and Reverend Miller stayed up until the wee small hours of the morning talking about work. Brad shared his chaplaincy duties and responsibilities with Reverend Miller and talked about all the many ICU room scenarios he had been involved in. He was excited to be moving back to Georgia and wanted to know Pastor Miller's feelings about First Baptist, McRae.

"Brad, one of my dearest friends in the ministry, Charles Webster, pastors the First United Methodist Church there in McRae. He and I were classmates at Candler School of Theology at Emory University in Atlanta. He will be a great mentor for you should you need help along the way. In fact, I'll give you his telephone number, and you could easily call and ask him his opinion about First Baptist. The two churches have always worked well together in the community, and they are only a couple of blocks apart. He'll be a great resource person for you. As you saw, the town is about the size of Fairaday, perhaps just a bit larger. I'm not sure where Anna Louise would secure work in her field of speech therapy, but I'm certain that if it be the Lord's Will, He'll make it happen. Just trust the Lord, Son, trust the Lord for the answer."

"Thank you, Pastor John. You've always been a guiding light for me and have supported me through everything I've sought to do. I'll certainly give Brother Webster a call and ask for his opinion as well. That will be most helpful, especially since I'll be working very closely with him on community activities, etc." Brad was very appreciative to Pastor Miller for his great insight and wisdom.

The girls were in the baby's room talking about everything under the sun. Margie was so happy about the prospects of having Anna Louise back in the area again and couldn't wait for them to move so she would be able to see little Bradley more often. It was at that point that Anna Louise brought more news to her mother, Margie.

"Mom, I wasn't sure when to tell you, but we're going to have number two! I'm about two months into the pregnancy now and was waiting for a special time to break the news to you and dad." Anna Louise didn't know how her mother would respond, so she sat anxiously waiting.

Margie threw her arms into the air and shouted "Hallelujah! Little Bradley's going to have a little sister!"

"Mom," Anna Louise invoked, "We do not know the gender of our baby at this point, so we cannot assume that little Bradley is going to have a sister. It may well be another brother, since boys run in Brad's family line."

"It doesn't matter, honey, I was only so exuberant with joy that it just came out of me. I would be more than happy with either one. We've got to tell your Dad. I know that he will be extremely happy with the news." Margie was elated with the news.

Brad had finally fallen asleep on the living room sofa in his Sunday suit. Pastor Miller had slipped off to his bed, so Margie would have to wait until morning to break the news to him. She and Anna Louise went to the spare bedroom and cuddled up together until morning.

At 6:00 AM, barely three hours from the time they had finally gone to bed, Margie Miller was up and cooking breakfast for the crew. When she had it ready, she went to the rooms down the hall to awaken Reverend Miller and Anna Louise. Brad was still on the couch and Mrs. Miller lightly touched him on the shoulder and awakened him.

At the breakfast table, Anna Louise made her wonderful and exciting announcement about her pregnancy. Brad also made his announcement in accepting the new pastorate in McRae. Everyone rejoiced and plans were made for the end of Brad's third year and their move to McRae.

Within a week's time, Anna Louise was notified of a position opening up in the fall with the Oconee Area Training Center for a speech therapist. The position was located twenty miles north of McRae in a town called Eastman. She would actually be covering six counties, and

Telfair, the county in which McRae was located, would be one of those. A member of the McRae First Baptist Church had made a phone call to the Director and told her of Anna Louise's previous work in Wake Forest and the fact that she and Brad were taking the pastorate at First Baptist. That's basically all it took for the Director to call and set up an interview with Anna Louise. She was so elated over having that hurdle out of the way; she made certain that the Director understood that she was with child. Brad had already contacted the head deacon at First Baptist in McRae and had agreed to take the position. Things were now set for the family to move at the end of May, following Brad's graduation.

Brad would have to resign his position at Oak Grove, complete his CPE work, and then attend graduation on May 21st before the move could transpire. Anna Louise would put in her resignation papers with the Nursing Home chain as well.

The Petersons and Millers came up for the graduation together, including Jason and his girlfriend from Florida. It was a beautiful day in so many ways, and again, Anna Louise again considered herself the luckiest girl in the world! Life is good, she thought. Everything was working out just great at this point. God was in His heaven, and all was right with the world. But who can ever predict the hands of fate? When that ugly and often-cruel hand moves upon the earth, it is often quick and sure, changing lives and destinies in a heartbeat. It is not concerned with the individual as much as it is with the common and mundane things of life, the ordinary that are overlooked along the way. Smooth sailing one day and then BANG! It happens. No warning. No reason. It's like a thief in the night who comes to steal away all that is held precious and dear. It doesn't really set its sights upon one person in particular, it just HAPPENS! A slip-up here, there, and before you are even aware, it happens. Fate!

Chapter Eighteen
An Old Enemy Returns

Tragic news came to the Millers and Petersons in late July. Anna Louise had a miscarriage and had to have the baby aborted at the Medical Center in Macon. Brad had rushed her there at the persistence of their new doctor in McRae. The family was devastated, and Anna Louise was so disheartened. It had been a little girl, which Anna Louise felt would have completed their perfect little family.

In late November of that same year, Anna Louise felt a gnawing pain in her right side. It was so severe that she immediately set-up an appointment with her local physician in McRae. After blood tests and a series of x-rays, he discovered a small tumor in her side. Her parents, who suggested a return to Emory Hospital in Atlanta, called to make her an appointment with Anna Louise's doctor.

Extensive tests ensued in the following days at Emory. Doctor Harry Messner, Head of Oncology at Emory, took on her case and placed Anna Louise immediately in a room and began extensive tests. A biopsy was done the second day while everyone in the family waited anxiously in the waiting room area. Two days later, the tests confirmed a reoccurrence of Anna Louise's leukemia. It had localized itself in the tumor this time around, and it was so near to her heart that it appeared inoperable at first. However, after further studies, surgery was scheduled immediately by Dr. Messner. They would simply have to take a chance because this was life-threatening to Anna Louise. The choice however, belonged to Brad and Anna Louise, a choice neither was capable of making at that point, so they called on their parents to help them in their decision.

Margie spoke first that day. "Honey, you know we're with you no matter which choice you make. We've always been there for you. This is just another one of those bumps in the road that God's going to smooth out. At least we should give the surgery a try, don't you think?"

"Dad," Anna Louise asked, with tears streaming down her face, "give me the final word. I need to hear it from you! You've always given me sound advice and I trust your final decision. What do you say? Should we have the surgery or just take the treatments and hope for the best?"

"My dear, Anna Louise, I can't be responsible for making that kind of decision alone. You are married now and are mature enough to make your own decisions. I think that you and Brad alone should decide, and we will support whatever choice you make. You know that, and we'll all be right here for you." Her father was almost in tears and his voice was shaky.

"Thank you, Dad. I somehow knew that you would have the right answer," Anna Louise said. She turned to Brad who was holding her right hand as she lay in the bed. "Folks," Anna said, "Could Brad and I have a few moments together, just the two of us? We've got some big stuff to talk about right now."

Everyone except Brad left the room for the waiting area while Brad and Anna Louise made their decision. It seemed like an eternity to the Petersons and the Millers, so it had to be agonizing for Anna Louise and Brad. What with the recent miscarriage, the moving in May to McRae, the new job in Eastman . . . Anna Louise definitely had a tough decision to make.

"Brad," Anna Louise called, "What are we going to do? You know I trust in you, honey, to help me in every respect, but I need your input at this point. This is a far greater decision than I am capable of making on my own. You are my soul mate, and I'm counting on you."

Brad took both of her hands and sat on the edge of

the bed with Anna Louise. He looked for the longest into her beautiful blue eyes and finally responded. "Anna Louise Miller, we are all in God's hands. We trust physicians to know what is right and proper, and Dr. Messner feels it vital to go in and remove the tumor at this point. I have faith in him and know that he will do the right thing. I also have a deep abiding faith in you and want you around with me for a few more years! I am not about to lose you, so I feel that surgery is the best route. We can worry about the chemo treatments later. Let's just get this thing done now!"

"Brad, I knew that I could count on you." Anna Louise's complexion changed completely as she gazed into the loving eyes of her sweet husband.

"O.K. then. Let's call the folks in and Dr. Messner and let them know what we've decided to do." Anna Louise had regained her confidence and was ready for the surgery.

The surgery with Dr. Messner came early the following morning and was a grueling six hours of extensive work, mainly because of the location of the tumor. The Petersons and Millers, along with several Macon, McRae, and Fairaday parishioners, filled the waiting area to overflowing. They had all come to Atlanta in support of this couple.

The surgery was a complete success. The tumor was removed and was followed by two weeks of radiation treatments just to be on the safe side. Anna Louise recuperated over the holidays and was able to return to her work in mid-January. No signs of the leukemia or tumor! What a blessing! God had worked yet another miracle in the life of Anna Louise Miller. She had once again escaped the cold hand of death, and she knew it! She was now in remission once again. The wheels of fate had tilted again in her favor, and life was once again good.

Chapter Nineteen
"My God, What a Mess!"

Raymond and Roscoe fought feverishly to hose down the car in the center of the road with little success. A crowd of approximately 30 to 40 people were standing around the wreck and watching the action. The front of the mid-sized car had been crushed into the front seat with such force that the person inside was unable to escape. The ambulance service had arrived, along with the fire trucks from Fitzgerald and Irwinville. A pickup truck was criss-cross the ditch on the right side of the road, and an elderly man was trapped inside. The steering wheel had broken, and the column itself had been driven through the man's chest, killing him instantly.

"My God, what a mess!" Roscoe said to Raymond. "I've never seen anything this tragic before in all these years of work. We gotta keep workin' on that fire, though, before it gets out of control."

Raymond spoke up and said, "Roscoe, you don't never know what's gonna happen around the next bend, do you? I've just had this feeling in my bones for the past couple of weeks that something tragic was going to happen in my life. Now I know what it is. I really feel sorry for these two people who met on this hillside in such a tragic fashion."

As the firemen worked non-stop on the car fire, a couple of Sheriff's deputies were using the Jaws-of-Life contraption to free the elderly man from his pickup. They were having a very difficult time, especially with the fire so close by, but eventually freed him from the truck and placed him in a brown body bag and put him in the back of the Fitzgerald ambulance. It would be approximately 20 minutes later when the fire in the car was extinguished. A wrecker had arrived, at the request of the Sheriff's department, and it hooked up to the car and pulled it to the roadside, once the flames were out. The rims of the tires made an awful screeching sound as the metal drove lines across the highway. The tires had all melted with the fire, and the interior of the car was gutted. There's no way that anyone could possibly have escaped in that vehicle. Death had to be instant and merciful.

There was a frightened chill on the faces of all people standing around the wreck, and the authorities were asking if anyone had witnessed the event. There was only one fellow there who could partially give a witness. He had not seen the actual crash but had been the first to arrive on the scene.

Roscoe and Raymond had to stay around long after everyone else had left to make certain the fire was completely out and there were no sparks that had made it to the surrounding wooded areas. They had to walk through the woods and scout things out before they could close the books on this one. They soon returned to Fitzgerald to their base headquarters, and the stories started growing about the incident. Everyone wanted to know if the two people involved in the wreck were from Fitzgerald. Roscoe had told them that the only I.D. was on the old man, and he was apparently from Simpson. He was driving a Pepsi-Cola pickup truck, and it was crushed like an accordion!

Chapter Twenty
Class Reunion

Anna Louise had a bouncing baby girl approximately two years after her surgery in Atlanta. It weighed 8 pounds, 2-1/2 ounces, and was 21 inches in length. It was a beautiful blonde headed, blue-eyed girl whom they named Melody Nichole Peterson. She was truly a delight from the very beginning. Just a bundle of perfect beauty and a wonderful baby. Anna Louise honored her dear friend Melody by giving the child her first name. Melody was so overwhelmed that she was just speechless when she received the news.

Brad was doing great at the McRae First Baptist Church. Lives were being saved and added almost weekly to the church. He even began working on extension studies to receive his Doctor of Divinity degree and would meet once a month with a group of his peers. They would study together from Friday morning until Saturday afternoon. This route would take him a couple of years to complete, but he felt the time was inconsequential. He was already doing what he loved to do, and his life's work was very fruitful. The studies simply complemented his daily work. He enjoyed being with the other peers as well, so Anna Louise would often just take off to her parents in Macon or down to Fairaday to the Petersons while Brad was gone. This gave the grandparents much pleasure.

Melody called Anna Louise one day and told her about plans for their Ten-Year Class Reunion in Fairaday. "You've gotta come, Anna Louise! I've promised every-body that you'd be here. Heath says that you're coming even if he has to come up there to McRae and get you! Say you'll come, dear. It will be so great seeing you again and reminiscing about the old days with our friends."

Anna Louise was excited about returning for the class reunion and began making serious plans. She would have to work that Friday morning in Eastman and couldn't leave until around 1:00 P.M. for Fairaday. Brad was plan-ning to go down to Fairaday early on Tuesday to spend a few days with his parents and would await Anna Louise's arrival on Friday evening. The children would be picked up by the Millers from Macon on Thursday and would not be in daycare on Friday. Everything seemed set for this wonderful weekend of frivolity and fun.

Anna Louise had several cases to see on Friday morning before she could depart from McRae. One of her clients was in Dublin, Georgia, about 35 miles from McRae, and it was pushing her to get back in time to leave for the reunion, but she made it. She packed her bags and left McRae around 1:15 PM and headed towards Fairaday. She was anxious to get there and to see her old friends.

She began to think back on all of the victories she had been able to win in her short life and felt truly blessed of God. She had the wonderful love of a family who had stood by her through so many encounters of sickness and disease. Her church families in Fairaday, Wake Forest, and McRae had been wonderful to them. The way her jobs just seemed to come from out of the blue and with perfect timing let her know that God was in control.

As Anna Louise passed over the Ocmulgee River bridge in Jacksonville and turned right towards Fitzgerald, she continued to reminisce about her precious little family God had blessed her with. They were complete now, she and Brad, since little Melody had entered their lives. Bradley and Melody were such sweet, sweet children, and she thanked God for them as she fought the evening sun in her face. With regrets to her father, Anna Louise thought that Brad was the better preacher, although she would never tell her father! Then there was Melody, her confidant and life-long friend. Melody had helped her through a lot, and she would soon be celebrating their tenth high school re-union, the first since their graduation. In just a few more hours, she would be back in Fairaday among family and friends. Life was good!

As Anna Louise drove through Fitzgerald, she stopped briefly at the local Magic-Mart and filled up her car and used the restroom. She purchased a Pepsi and a honey bun to give her a little boost for the rest of the journey. Mr. Killdare, store manager, started a conversation with her, noticing the beautiful cross around Anna

Louise's neck. It was hand-carved and had been given to her on the occasion of her 7th grade graduation by Mr. Clyde Durrence, a long-time member of the Fairaday United Methodist Church. Mr. Durrence had carved many animal figures and trinkets out of Okefeenokee Swamp Cypress knees. Those are the roots that grow out of the swamp from the base of cypress trees, and the grain of wood and color make for beautiful carvings. Mr. Durrence would sell these figurines and carvings at local flea markets around in the area.

"Howdy, Miss. I couldn't help but notice your beautiful cross. Had it long?" Mr. Killdare asked.

"Quite a while, sir," Anna Louise responded. "I've been wearing it since the Seventh grade! A dear friend carved it just for me as a present at my Seventh grade graduation. It has actually started many conversations for me over the years, and I've been able to share my faith with folks because of this cross."

"That's an interesting story, young lady. Are you from around these parts?" he asked.

"Not any more, but I used to live in Fairaday a few years ago. I guess you could say that I grew up there since my father was the pastor of the Methodist Church in Fairaday for twenty years." Anna Louise spoke of her father's twenty years in one church with great pride.

"Wow! That's an unusual number of years for a pastor to be in a Methodist Church, ain't it?" Mr. Killdare asked.

"Yes sir, it is. But my father is a most unusual pastor! He's the most wonderful man in all the world. He is keeping my children up in Macon this weekend while I return to Fairaday for my 10-year Class Reunion." Anna Louise's excitement must have shown through to Mr. Killdare.

"Sounds like you're going to have a great weekend, dear. You be careful out there on this State Highway. Never know what's around the next bend."

With that, Anna Louise returned to her car and headed west towards Fairaday. A few miles outside of town, after finishing her Pepsi and honey bun, she began to feel a bit dizzy. She pulled off the roadside for a few moments until the feeling passed. She turned on the car stereo and listened to a tape by Amy Grant. She was singing along with Amy and thinking of Fairaday, Melody and Heath, Brad and the children, her parents . . . She topped the hill ahead of her, which curved back to the left, and …

Chapter Twenty One
The Finale

John Maxwell raced to the sight at the top of the hill beyond the river bridge. Everything seemed a blur to him as he sped up the highway to the wreckage. Sure enough, his fears were confirmed. It had been a head-on collision between a small pickup truck and a mid-sized car just on his side of the hill. The truck had been forced backwards across the ditch to his right and looked like a compressed accordion. The car was still crossways in the middle of the two lanes of blacktop asphalt. Steam was pouring out of both engines, and John feared an explosion would occur at any moment.

John pulled his car off the right side of the road and rushed over to the pickup truck. An older gentleman was behind the wheel, and John reached in to check for a pulse on his neck. Unable to find one, he then noticed that the steering wheel had broken off and its column had been plunged through the older man's chest. Terrible sight, John thought, his stomach feeling very queasy and his adrenalin pumping rapidly throughout his body.

No time to waste, John thought. This is a danger-ous situation here on the hill and another car may be on its way at any moment, not knowing what's on the other side. With that, John started moving to the center of the road towards the car involved in the accident. About ten feet away, he noticed a young lady's head leaning against the driver's side window. It was then that he heard a sizzling sound, and, by instinct, he backed away thinking that the gas tank was about to explode. It did, and, as the explo-sion rocked the quietness of the countryside, it knocked John off his feet and back to the edge of the road. By that time, two other cars had approached the scene, and people had gotten out to help. John was quite shaken, and an older fellow came over to him and helped him to his feet, away from the flames of the car. By that time, it was too late to save the lady in the car. A couple in a blue Chevro-let came by and stopped where John and the elderly gen-tleman stood and asked if they could do anything. John sent them on up the road to Irwinville and asked them to get help there at a store. John went out into the highway on the other side of the hill to help direct traffic. Two other men had arrived and were doing the same on the op-posite side of the hill.

Within twenty minutes, a forestry fire truck arrived along with an ambulance from Ben Hill County. The Jaws of Life instrument was used to free the elderly man in the Pepsi-Cola pickup truck. He was bagged and placed on a stretcher and loaded into the back of the ambulance. The car was still on fire and had burned a deep rut into the

smoldering asphalt underneath. John could smell the awful stench of burning flesh and saw that young lady's face
over-and-over again a million times in his mind as he continued to direct traffic. He could never forget the face!

After about an hour, the forestry fire truck had the
fire extinguished and a wrecker arrived to pull the burned
vehicle over to the roadside so that traffic on the highway
could resume. Cars had been backed up for miles, people
wondering what was going on. As soon as possible, the
emergency medical people began to look for signs of what
was left of a body in the vehicle, once the Jaws of Life
pried the driver's side door open. I watched as the EMT's
scooped up a couple of handfuls of human flesh and bone
from the floor of the vehicle, directly underneath the steering wheel. That was all that was left of someone's life, a
couple of handfuls of flesh and bone!

Who was this? John wondered. What was her
story? How did she arrive at this fateful place on this fateful afternoon? What had brought her here to meet her demise?

John then thought of the old man in the pickup.
What's his story? Apparently he had worked for the
Pepsi-Cola Company and had a couple of canisters in the
back of his truck. Where was he going? What brought him
here to meet his demise?

The wreck was soon cleared from the roadway,
and all of the emergency vehicles and workers had left.
John sat in his car, feeling deep remorse, wondering how
soon it would take for the families of these two people to

be notified about their deaths. He looked again at the spot of the collision. Skid marks! Those marks symbolized the tragedy of what had just occurred at the hands of fate. Families and lives would be forever changed after today, and certainly, John Maxwell's life would never be the same!

A couple of forestry people came walking over to John's car and began asking him questions. "Did you see the whole thing?" a person named Roscoe asked.

"No sir. I just saw the aftermath of the wreck, seconds after it had occurred, and raced up here to check on things." John's voice was shaking. "Ain't never seen anything like this in my life, and I hope and pray that I won't see anything like it again!"

"Son, did you see who was in the car?" John could see his name badge was Raymond.

"Yes sir. I saw a young woman, maybe in her early thirties with her head against the driver's side window. The car started to sizzle before I could get closer, so I backed off just before it blew." John stated.

John had to travel that same route every day for the rest of his college career, even passing that way through Tifton to Valdosta State for two years. Each morning and afternoon, he would slow down and briefly pause at the site of the wreck, remembering that sacred spot where two lives meshed for time and eternity, two lives that were very special and dear to those who knew and loved them. John still remembers the smell of burning flesh and often awakens in the middle of the night in cold sweats.

Fate? Maybe so. But who can say? One will never be sure of what it is that brings certain lives together at a particular point and place in time. There are intersections everywhere; some of them are blind, some visible, where crosses the busyness of our lives.

State Highway 92 has long since been repaved, but a small cross on the roadside still marks the spot where it happened. I have watched, from time to time when passing, and have noticed when new flowers have been brought there to surround the cross. That cross represents someone, somebody who once lived a vibrant and active life, but is no more.

Where does the love of God go when the minutes, hours, days, months and years turn into mere seconds of time? Only a brief moment in time, and it's all over!

The next time you're traveling down the highway and notice skid marks on the road or a little white cross by the side of the road, show a little more respect. When you see those marks, say a prayer and thank God that you're still counted among the living!